I0525271

Warren Pieces

The Many Loves of a Slightly Old, Slightly Stout, Slightly Bald Raconteur

And Other Stories

MIDDLETON
Books

This is a publication of Middleton Books
832 Dana Drive, Coatesville, PA 19320
USA
www.middletonbooks.com

©2015 by Jonathan D. Scott
All rights reserved

ISBN 978-0-9716611-7-2
Printed in the United States of America

Without limiting the rights under copyright reserved
above, no part of this publication may be reproduced,
stored in or introduced into a retrieval system, or
transmitted, in any form or by any means (electronic,
mechanical, photocopying, recording, or otherwise),
without prior written permission of both the copyright
owner and the above publisher.

This is a work of fiction.
Any resemblance to actual persons is entirely coincidental.

Author's Note

It has come to my attention that some upstart Russian has published a novel with a title that sounds peculiarly similar to this work. This has lately become the source of much confusion in the publishing world.

I have in my possession a tear-stained note from a secondary school teacher in Billings, Montana who ordered 27 copies of my book for her Advanced Literature class. Imagine her dismay on the first day of school finding instead a box of 1,296-page books about, of all things, the French invasion of Russia during the Napoleonic Era.

One — obviously confused — reviewer, describing my book as "one of the most important works of world literature," attributed it not to *Warren Pieces*, but to this damned Russian's sound-alike.

I intend to bring a stiff lawsuit. That is, if I can ever get an attorney to return my phone calls.

J.D.S.

"The Biblio Files"
first published in *Still Crazy*, May 2008

"First Course Affair"
first published in *Writers' Post Journal*, June 2007

"Turn On Tune In"
first published in *Stymie*, June 2007

"Political Camp Pains"
first published in *Abandoned Towers*, July 2009

All other Warren Pieces first published on
www.pikerpress.com, 2009-2013

"Mixed Messages"
first published on www.storyglossia.com, March 2006

"The Man Who Invented Polka Dots"
first published on www.samizdada.com, February 2007

"Ever So Slightly Mangled"
first published in *Skyline Magazine*, Fall 2007

"The Miraculous Powers of Missy McKinnick"
first published in *Duck and Herring Pocket Field Guide*,
Summer 2007

"Dieting With Jesus"
first published on www.johnnyamerica.net, June 2006

CONTENTS

WARREN PIECES

The Biblio Files

"I've never heard of grown man afraid of going into a bookstore." The man in the black Gortex jacket stands in a circle of light on the top of brick steps, holding open a glass door.

"I'll just wait here for you." The other man is slightly older, slightly stouter and slightly balder. He turns up the collar of a wrinkled raincoat.

"It's raining," says the man in the black Gortex jacket.

"I'll be fine."

The man in the Gortex jacket lets the door close. "You surprise me, Warren. I always took you for an intellectual type — the sort who would hang around in bookstores all day. Why can't you come in with me for a moment?"

"It's not that I can't. It's just that I'd rather not." Warren takes off his glasses and wipes them on the sleeve of his coat. "Around the next block is a small but comfortable drinking establishment. If you would be so kind as to buy me a glass of Bourgogne, I will be more than happy to relate the entire bitter tale that explains why."

The man in the Gortex jacket laughs. "No wonder they say you're an oddball, Warren."

"Who says that?"

"Just a couple of guys," says the man in the black Gortex jacket.

* * *

I used to live in an apartment (says Warren) which was just eight blocks from City Library, which housed a superb collection of old volumes and classic literature. The truth is, I can't tolerate popular contemporary literature. I once tried to read a paperback that I found in the train. It was about a woman who — and I'm not exaggerating even slightly — was unable to choose between a wealthy, shallow man who had not matured past adolescence and an impecunious, shallow man who had not matured past adolescence. The book's main attraction, as far as I could speculate, was the repetitive use of the adjectives 'hot,' 'sweaty,' and 'gargantuan.'

That is why I became a collector of old books. I spent a great deal of time searching for authors who inspired me sufficiently to collect rare copies of their works. This search often took me to City Library, and that is why I happened to be there on the evening of Wednesday, November 10th.

I paused for a moment between the sections on Modern Central Asian Religious Dialectics and Political Diatribes of Nineteenth Century Micronesia when a woman approached and addressed me. As I have never been the sort of man with whom strange women strike up conversations, I was taken aback. She had a green plastic card pinned to her polyester-blend sweater with the words LILLIAN SMITH, COLLECTIONS LIBRARIAN in raised letters.

"May I help you?" she asked.

I couldn't recall seeing her before, however hers was not a particularly memorable face. She was of medium height and build, her hair a medium brown, with a pair of medium eyes behind glasses that seemed more appropriate for a woman twice her age.

"I doubt you could help me," I told her. I prefer not to discuss my predelictions with strangers.

"You look like the sort of man who has sophisticated tastes in reading," she replied.

I wasn't about to lie. "Well, yes," I said. "In fact I'm something of an amateur collector of rare books."

"Well, you have nothing to apologize for," she said, although the idea of apologizing hadn't — and would never have — occurred to me. "I find book collectors to be among the most interesting people in the world."

I was about to ask her if she didn't have some re-shelving project to keep her occupied, when something seemingly insignificant occurred which set off an extraordinary series of events that was to change both our lives. She smiled and touched my hand. It was merely a light touch, but of sufficient pressure to make me realize I hadn't been touched by a woman in a very long time, the last being at an office Christmas party when an intoxicated receptionist tweaked my nose.

"I enjoy collecting rare books myself," she said. "There's something about holding an old book that fires one's imagination, don't you think? What its history has been, who has read it and left his mark on the pages, on whom the book has left a mark."

I wasn't able to prevent myself from looking at her hand. She had a stout wrist with fine hair — qualities that I have always found to be stimulating in a woman. Further, I noticed that below her modestly long skirt, she had wonderfully sturdy ankles above sensible red and white athletic shoes.

Despite my usual reticence with women, I plunged ahead into the conversation. "A few years ago I began collecting the works of O. Henry, which I'm sure you will recognize as the *nom de plume* of author William Sydney Porter. I have a 1923 first edition soft cover of a selection of his stories signed by his daughter, Margaret Porter Cesare. It reads, *"Pop loved life, and his death was a real surprise ending."*

Her brown eyes grew wide behind her glasses, and I observed that they carried a certain appealing light in spite of a noticeable thinness of lash.

"Then I became interested in James — Henry James, of course," I continued. "One of the finest writers in the English language. The highlight of my James collection is an 1886 first edition of *The Bostonians*, signed by the author with a personal note, presumably to Harriet Beecher Stowe, *"Harriet, you write damn well for a dame."*

I could tell the woman was impressed.

"Most recently, after reading *A Portrait of the Artist as a Young Man*, I undertook a search for collectors' editions of James Joyce. My most treasured possession is a limited edition, leather-bound copy of *Ulysses*. It was discovered propping up an unbalanced bar table in a Dublin pub. The mark of the leg is still visible."

At that point I realized I was gasconading to an inappropriate degree. "Actually, the remainder of my collection is rather meager, I'm afraid. I'm very much in the process of acquisition."

She brought her fingers to her chin, and tilted her head. "O. Henry, Henry James, James Joyce. Hmmm. You might give Joyce Carol Oates a try. I have an inscribed copy of her first published book, *By the North Gate*. It had been a gift to her plumber. She wrote, *"Thanks for fixing my crapper. Toodle-oo, Joyce."*

"My goodness," I said. My head was beginning to swim.

"Perhaps" she said, "you would be interested in hearing about other books in my collection."

"Interested? Yes, certainly I'm interested. In fact, I'm exceedingly interested."

"I'm Lillian." She said, offering me her right hand.

"Warren Borman." She placed her left hand on top of mine and smiled at me once again. "It is a pleasure to meet you, Mr. Borman."

"Please do call me Warren."

"And please do call me, Warren," she said, laughing. Once I had caught the humor of her remark, I laughed also.

I wrote her phone number on the back of my library card and arranged to have dinner with her on the coming Friday evening.

In the space of a very moments I had become utterly and irreversibly smitten.

* * *

The next morning after showering, I happened to glance at the full-length mirror on my bathroom door. It is an act I usually avoid for good reason. I resolved that I would skip breakfast that morning, possibly lunch, and perhaps even dinner. I began to wonder how much weight a middle-aged man could lose in thirty-seven hours.

Later I found myself sitting in the cafeteria of my office building trying to extract as much nutrition as I could from slightly flavored soda water. "If you were taking an attractive woman out to dinner," I asked a fellow from Research and Development, "where would you go?"

He looked at me and spoke in the charming idiom of a South Philadelphia native. "If I was taking a fucking attractive woman out to fucking dinner and my fucking old lady found out, I'd go fucking straight to fucking hell, that's where I'd go. Why, you got a fucking date, Warren?"

I told him that indeed I did.

"Well here's a piece of advice, and I won't even charge you for it. Get yourself some pomade, grease up what you've got left of hair, and comb it across that dome of yours. Only women that are freaks go for bald men."

I thanked him.

"You're fucking welcome," he said.

* * *

The next day I went shopping for a new suit. You well can imagine my disappointment when I discovered that in spite of my austerities, I still required 42-inch trousers. However, I purchased a suit the color of a day-old bruise and a maroon tie that sported small yellow horseshoes. I was feeling devil-may-care.

I arrived at the door of Lillian's apartment at exactly 7:58 and pushed an eager finger on the buzzer.

"You are very prompt, Warren," she said, slipping out of her door. "I appreciate that in a man."

"And I appreciate a woman who appreciates prompt-ness in a man," I said, trying inconspicuously to ensure that my well-oiled hair was still in place.

Beneath a fuzzy brown coat she wore a pink dress with orange flowers that demurely concealed her figure. On her ears were two faux-jeweled pink earrings and in her hair two pink plastic clips.

"You look lovely this evening," I told her.

"Warren," she said, "you are far too kind." The ruddy blush that rose to her cheeks perfectly complemented her ensemble.

"Not nearly kind enough for you," I said, rather neatly.

* * *

I had made reservations at Bookbinder's Seafood which at that time was considered the finest restaurant in the city. When the pompous *maitre'dhotel* finally left us alone to peruse our menus, my eyes lit upon a description of the evening special, *Langoustine a la Venus de Milo*. My stomach, deprived of food for two days, reacted almost instantly, giving everyone in the vicinity the impression that a mild thunderstorm had formed inside the restaurant.

"Are you all right, Warren?" Lillian whispered, politely attempting to mitigate my embarrassment.

"All right? Unquestionably all right. In fact, in anticipating this evening, *'O then I was happy; O then each breath tasted sweeter — and I knew that my food would nourish me more,'* " I quoted. "Walt Whitman."

She was visibly impressed at my erudition. However, she was not to be outdone. "One of my collected volumes I treasure most," she said, "is an early David McKay edition of Whitman, inscribed to his boyfriend, J. Addington Symonds. He wrote, *"Thanks for the suggestion. Much better title than* Leaves of Cabbage.*"*

And so the evening went. When not paying attention to my *Langoustine*, I was enthralled by her knowledge of rare books. We discussed everything from a Gutenberg Bible with *Second Thessalonians* printed upside down to a copy of Kerouac's *On the Road* that had once belonged to Pope John Paul I. We lost all track of time, and it was only when our waiter told us there was no more coffee, and would be no more until the following evening, that I paid for the meal, left two dollar bills on the table, and proceeded to take Lillian back to her apartment.

"Warren," she whispered as we sat double-parked in front of her building, "would you like to come up and see my collection?"

I was charged with excitement. "Lillian, I would like nothing more."

She began searching the car interior and then exclaimed, "Oh, hell's bells, I must have left my purse in the restaurant."

"No need to fret, my dear. I'll simply call Bookbinders and have them ensure its safety until we can retrieve it."

"There's no need to do that, Warren. I left a spare key in the straw of the artificial palm tree at the end of my hallway."

"Nonsense," I said, pulling out the cellular phone provided by my employers. "We must recover your wallet and your identification papers. There is widespread concern regarding the crime of identify theft."

Within moments I had the manager on the line. "Sir, my name is Borman — Warren Borman. My date and I were patrons of your establishment this evening, and we seem to have left behind a purse. It is chartreuse faux-leather with brown fringe and a broken strap. We will be there in a few moments."

"Warren…," she said.

"You don't have to thank me, Lillian. It is merely the duties of a *preux chevalier* on behalf of his lady."

True to my word, we were back at Bookbinders within a few moments. Due to the late hour, the employees were busily cleaning the premises and preparing to close. The manager met us at the door. "I am terribly sorry, Mr. Borman. We scoured the restaurant from top to bottom and the purse you describe is not here. I would be shocked to learn that any of our patrons or employees might have stolen it, but I've taken the liberty to notify the police."

"We are grateful, sir," I said.

"Oh, my," said Lillian.

It was just then that one of the City's finest arrived with the purse in hand. "I retrieved the stolen article from a man attempting to enter a black BMW in a parking garage at Sixth and Chestnut. The perpetrator is a city councilman with an untreated case of kleptomania. He is now in custody."

"Are you Lillian Smith?" he asked her.

She nodded.

"Lillian Smith, alias Lillian O'Callahan, alias Lillian Wong, alias Lillian Manischewitz?"

She began to cry. No, to be more exact, she began to sob.

I was furious. "What is the meaning of this?"

"This woman is wanted in seventeen states for grand larceny. She uses fake credentials to obtain jobs in libraries and absconds with valuable books. She's known to the FBI as 'Library Lil.'"

"Lillian," I asked, "is this true?"

She didn't answer, only continued to sob, presenting open arms to be handcuffed. She was.

When the officer had finished reciting a litany of

criminal civil rights, Lillian turned to me with tear-stained cheeks. "Warren, we could have made the perfect-bound couple."

I felt a stab in my heart, as if I had forever lost all capacity to love. "'Of all sad words of tongue or pen," I said, "'the saddest are *what might have been.'* Omar Khayyam."

As the gendarme led her off, Lillian called out over her shoulder. "If only I could show you my copy of *The Rubaiyat* translated into Ebonics."

* * *

"The next week," Warren says to his companion, "I sold my entire library on eBay. I could no longer bear the sight of it. With the proceeds I bought a large-screen, high-definition television. Now I spend my lonely evenings watching reality programs."

His companion stands and reaches for the black Gortex jacket that hangs on the back of the chair. "Library Lil? Are you putting me on, Warren?"

Warren also stands, puts a quarter on the table, and smiling, dons his wrinkled raincoat.

A First Course Affair

A slender man with a square jaw and an Ashworth diamond-weave sweater walks into the Oak Terrace clubhouse, wiping an errant bead of sweat from his forehead with a handkerchief. As he walks up to the bar he notices a slightly stouter, slightly older, and slightly balder man sitting in an easy chair facing the eighteenth green. "Warren," he says to seated man, "how come you're not playing with the rest of us?"

Warren puts down a copy of *The Condê Nast Traveler* and an empty beer glass. "I won't play golf," he says.

The man in the Ashworth sweater smiles. "Oh, come on, Warren. It's just a company outing. Nobody really cares how well you do. Besides, there are lots of beginners out there. Just because you've never played…"

"What makes you assume I've never played?"

"You're just…ah, well, I don't know," the young man says, fumbling with his handkerchief. "It's just you don't seem the type."

"The type? What sort of type is that?"

"I...I just supposed —"

"Well, your supposition is incorrect. But if you agree to buy me another of these excellent Guinness Stouts, I will explain all and maybe find it in my heart to forgive your rudeness."

* * *

Things may have changed (says Warren), but at the time I was hired, our company required all new employees to undergo a complete physical examination. There are few things that I abhor more than being subjected to the indignities of modern medicine. However I was in dire need of employment so I acquiesced.

After the hordes of subordinate practitioners had completed their prodding and probing, an MD with the look of a man who knows no superior cornered me in the changing room. "Mr. Borman," he said, addressing my exposed hindquarters, "do you live an active life?"

I pulled up my boxers and thought it over. "Yes, of course. I have numerous pursuits that keep me intellectually quite active."

"No. I'm talking about keeping physically active. Exercise."

I was astonished. "Surely you're not referring to those repetitive tortures in which the self-obsessed indulge for the sake of their vanity."

He tapped the stethoscope that adorned his neck. "There are plenty of ways of being physically active without repetitive exercise," he said. "Sports, for example."

I had heard of sports. I knew that entire sections of daily newspapers were devoted to the subject. But I had never considered that normal people actually participated in such things. I told him so.

"Well, here's the straight story, Mr. Borman. Your weight, your blood pressure and your cholesterol levels are unacceptable for a man your age. If you don't want to exercise, you must get involved in some sort of sport or I'll refuse to approve you for employment."

"But…" I began.

"Come back in a week with evidence of a change of lifestyle or you'll get your exercise standing in the unemployment line."

* * *

The next day found me browsing through glossy magazines in the sports section of the newsstand at Market Street Station. The prospects appeared less than sanguine. Basketball required substantial height, a quality I have always been proud not to possess. Football players needed protuberant shoulders and Neanderthal foreheads. Boxing apparently involved inflicting pain on another to avoid having pain inflicted upon oneself, something that seemed needlessly unpleasant. Tennis, slightly more civilized, necessitated baring one's lower legs in public. Then, by chance, a copy of *Golf Digest* fell on the floor.

Picking it up with the intention of replacing it on the shelf, I began thumbing through it with increasing interest. It appeared that all one did in playing golf was to stand still and hit a ball with a stick. The inventors of the game had mercifully provided for self-propelled vehicles to carry the golfers from location to location. What could be easier?

According to a Mr. Nicklaus, the finest in equipment was a set of Callaway Fusion FT-5 clubs. And according to a Mr. Woods, a pair of Foot Joy Power Platform Total Traction shoes was essential for success. Three dollars and ninety-nine cents later I betook myself, magazine in hand, to the nearest sporting goods store. In a few moments I had reached my credit card spending limit but had acquired all that was necessary to become a first-rate golfer.

* * *

"I would like to make a reservation," I said, having reached the local golf professional on the phone.

"You mean a tee time?" he asked.

"Tea time?" I was bewildered. "I am not concerned with refreshments. I wish to arrange to play golf."

"Aha. So when does your foursome want to tee off?"

I told him that I was so well equipped I didn't need a foursome.

"I'm sorry, sir," he said. "The only time we can accommodate a single player would be after five on a weekday."

"So be it," I said. "Put me down for tomorrow on your best first hole."

* * *

My initial swing was a slight disappointment. My most expensive and largest club failed to make contact with the ball. But we Bormans are known for our tenacity and commitment. By my fifth attempt I sent the ball flying in a most impressive arc that landed it several yards into a dense woods. The trouble I quickly determined was that the designer of the course had placed an obvious out-of-bounds terrain in range of a first swing.

Of course, I could not be blamed for his failing. So, not wishing to take the chance of soiling my Arnold Palmer 300-thread count, 100% cotton golf trousers, I chalked up the ball to an inevitable business loss. Unfortunately on Number Two I experienced a similar disappointment. This time the designer had apparently neglected to observe that a small pond lay between the starting point and the hole. It was an inexcusable mistake and one that I paid for with the loss of several balls that managed to make it as far as the water but no farther.

I had obviously chosen a defective course on which to play.

By the fifth hole I had only a single ball remaining. I had developed sufficient skill that a majority of the time I was able to make contact with it on my first attempt. The ball rose into high into the air and came to rest in the garden of a white Cape Cod style home perched on a small rise beside the course.

Being faced with a choice between playing the succeeding thirteen holes without a ball or retrieving mine, I drove up to the house. As I approached, my olfactory senses were met with a delicious aroma that was nothing less than intoxicating. I recognized it at once.

A slightly plump woman was sitting at a glass-topped table on her veranda, enjoying an evening meal.

"A thousand pardons for this unseemly intrusion, madam, but by chance would that be *Le Tian De Courgettes Aux Fruits De Mer* upon which you are dining?"

She dabbed at her mouth with a pressed cloth napkin. "Why, yes it is. How did you know?"

"French cuisine is one of my passions. I once had the pleasure of watching Mademoiselle Jacotte Brazier prepare that very dish on a television program."

"Isn't that something? I studied under Jacotte in Lyons for six months before I was married."

"Good Lord!" The pungent aroma of the seafood was making me lightheaded. "And here you are now living beside this very golf course," I said forcing my eyes from her plate to her face, which, I was discovering, was full but not unattractive. "You must be an aficionado of the sport."

"Not in the least. It was my husband who wanted to live here. My late husband, that is."

"Dear me."

"Now I just enjoy watching the hordes of poor suckers drive themselves into fits over this silly game." She smiled. "No offense."

"None taken," I said, noticing a pleasant bright sparkle in her deep brown eyes. My heart quickened. I had never before been that close to someone who could prepare *Le Tian De Courgettes*.

"By the way," she said, "my name is Sylvia Hillman."

"Warren Borman," I said with a slight bow.

"Your ball, Warren."

"Pardon me?"

"It rolled under the forsythia."

"Ah, yes. Well, I won't detain you from your meal any further, Mrs. Hillman. The professional was adamant that I return the vehicle in time for him to attend his young son's scholastic theatrical debut."

"Well, good luck with your round, Warren," she said, tucking in her napkin.

"Goodbye, Mrs. Hillman." My heart joined my stomach in an ache of emptiness as I retrieved my ball. The encounter had awakened in me more than one appetite.

* * *

It occurred to me that there was no reason to further risk losing my only remaining ball. I adopted a policy of driving right up to the hole, extending my arm, and dropping the ball. I was successful every time.

"So how was your score?" asked the professional as I returned to the clubhouse.

"My score?"

"Yes. How many strokes?" He studied my blank expression. "How many times did you hit the ball?"

I mentally made a tally. "Twelve," I said, a blush of shame rising to my cheeks. "Next time I'm certain I shall increase the number significantly."

He scratched his chin. "Listen, Mr. Borman. This

weekend we're having a novice golfers' tournament. You might find it helpful to go out with other players. The entrance fee is only $36 and the prize for the fewest number of strokes is a trophy and two prime rib dinners at the clubhouse restaurant.

I considered it. With little effort I could easily miss the ball more frequently than hitting it. Bringing a trophy to show to that insufferable MD would secure my prospects for employment. And secondly, but certainly no less, I hadn't had the pleasure of eating two prime ribs at one sitting since the previous New Years Eve.

"Where do I sign on?" I asked.

* * *

The following Saturday dawned full of sun and promise. I had been assiduously studying my copy of *Golf Digest.* I discovered an inventive method of hitting the ball close to the hole that a Mr. Mickelson enjoyed calling a "putt." I also learned that the key to success on the golf course was a winning attitude. So it was with such a frame of mind that I donned my stylish cap with several brand name emblems on the front, and arrived at the course.

"Ah, Mr. Borman." The professional buttonholed me in the midst of the throng. "I've put you in a special foursome. I'd like you to meet Mr. Weems, Mr. Smethurst, and Mr. Kowalick."

Weems, a fellow of slight proportions whose ninetieth birthday was a dim memory, gazed blankly into the distance through his spectacles and extended his hand, missing me by a good forty-five degrees. Smethurst was unable to shake my hand at all as his right arm was in a sling. Kowalick, however, a man with a build resembling a concrete bunker, easily made up for the other men's disabilities by squeezing my hand until the blood drained from my fingers.

"I've given you fellows the privilege of teeing off last," said the professional cheerfully. "That way you won't be bothered by other golfers behind you." He gave Weems a pat on the back that made the nonagenarian totter. "Have fun and may the best man win."

The prospects of that best man being myself became immediately apparent. Weems, when he was able to determine the approximate direction of the hole, hit his ball a good eight or ten feet. Smethurst, using only his left arm, reached distances approaching half that. And Kowalick, who I had expected to be the best of the group, seemed to unable to hit the ball at all. The man had arms of massive girth that expanded as he bore down on his swing, a swing that gouged a swath in the earth the size of a soldier's foxhole. The ball, however, remained stoically where he had placed it. Swearing loudly at the ball and himself, he would repeat the action with yet more energy, the effect being a wider and even deeper hole.

I must admit that my recent studies along with my winning attitude had given me enough skill at the game to have little patience with these incompetents. In a brief twenty strokes I had placed the ball in the hole and sat waiting for the others to catch up, thinking long, hard thoughts on the rules that permitted bumblers to play with superior players.

I therefore took it upon myself to forge onward on foot. I had the foresight to bring extra balls with me and lost fewer than six or eight on each of the second, third, and fourth holes. I could hear the intermittent bass curses of Kowalick far behind me as I strode up to take my first swing at the fifth. At the very top of my swing, the Callaway Fusion F5 Number 2 fell from my hand. Unmistakably, my nostrils were being seduced by the delicate saffron aroma of *Le Carré D'Agneau au Safran, Échalotes Confites.* I abandoned my clubs and trod to the white Cape Cod house on the hill.

There she was, the slightly rotund but ravishing figure of Mrs. Hillman —- perhaps the only woman in a radius of two hundred miles capable of creating such a dish. "Oh, Warren," she said, visibly brightening at my approach. "I was hoping that was you. I'm afraid I've made far more *Le Carré D'Agneau* than I can possibly eat. Would you care to join me?"

My eyes filled to the extent that I was afraid I might weep. "Mrs. Hillman, there is nothing in this world that would give me more pleasure. Are you certain it would not be an imposition?"

"Not at all. I was frustrated my entire married life. My husband's idea of haute cuisine was McDonald's special sauce. Sharing my cooking talents with a man who appreciates fine French food is a real pleasure. Here, let me get you a plate."

She returned from the house, the slight waddle in her stride exciting my passion. She ladled a portion of her creation onto an exquisite porcelain plate and set it in front of me. I loathe to attempt to describe the ecstatic state my first bite brought me. It was pure ambrosia, should ambrosia be made from lamb, saffron, and shallots.

"Do you like it?" she asked. I was touched at the expression of hopeful expectation on her angelic face.

"My dear lady, no man with an ounce of gustatory sensitivity could help but be swept up in utter infatuation with a woman of your consummate skill." I took off my cap and held it over my left breast. "I must be honest with you. I am but a currently unemployed accountant, but my prospects are good. Mrs. Hillman —- Sylvia —- I realize I may be exceeding the boundaries of social propriety, but one day, might you consider plighting your troth with mine?"

She stood beside me, heaping more lamb on my plate. "Oh, Warren, I've longed to meet a man who would appreciate me with such passion. And don't worry about money. My husband left me a bundle. We can travel the world together sampling the finest food from every culture and continent." With that she leaned over me, her soft breath coming ever closer to the bald spot on my head until I could fairly feel her moistened lips poised to kiss my waiting pate.

Just then there was a sound that rent the expectant stillness as if with a butcher's knife. A small white object hurled through the air with the force of a missile, rising from the fairway below and making instant impact with the back of Sylvia's neck. Kowalick had finally made contact with the ball.

*   *   *

"I sat with her until the ambulance arrived and rode with her to the hospital," says Warren to the man in the Ashworth sweater. "The emergency room physician gave me the tragic news. Sylvia would be just fine, but would remember nothing past her high school junior prom. She would not recognize me and, worst of all, never be able to cook a French meal again."

"Oh, come on, Warren. Do you expect me—"

"I was unspeakably heartbroken. I went home and immediately donated my Callaway Fusion FT-5 clubs, my Foot Joy Power Platform Total Traction shoes, my Arnold Palmer 300-thread count golf trousers, my cap, and my two remaining balls to the Boy Scouts. I've never been able to set foot upon a golf course again."

The man in the Ashworth sweater shakes his head. "I don't know, Warren. It sounds pretty bizarre to me. Of course, if it did happen, I'm awfully sorry."

"It runs quite deep," says Warren, handing his companion an empty glass. "But if you would care to buy me another of these excellent Guinness Stouts, I'm sure the pain would be substantially ameliorated."

Romancing Mom

"Who the hell was that?" A tall, slim man wearing a North Face jacket steps into the crosswalk, speaking over his shoulder to his lagging companion — a slightly shorter, slightly stouter, and slightly balder man.

"Only some people," the companion answers.

"What do you mean by 'only some people,' Warren? How do you get off knowing anyone who rides around town in a limo?"

"It's just as I said. Only some people. Some people I used to know. Let's leave it at that."

"Let's not leave it at that," says the man in the North Face jacket. "I'm not going to have lunch with a guy who leaves it at that."

Warren smiles. "If you would agree to pick up the tab for our upcoming meal," he says, "I will relate the entire sordid affair."

* * *

It began a great many years ago (says Warren), when I had

a position in the accounting department of Schmeltzer Industries. The Elder Mr. Schmeltzer had died of an aneurysm six months prior to my taking employment, and the business had fallen under the ownership of his son, the Younger Mr. Schmeltzer. The Younger Mr. Schmeltzer was full of all the callow zeal of a recent graduate of the Wharton School of Business. He seemed intent on disturbing the onerous but familiar status quo — the delightful grist for our mill of daily complaints in the company break room.

For example, it was not in the memory of the most experienced employee, an African-American gentleman named Jedediah Jones, that the Elder Mr. Schmeltzer had ever spoken to him in over thirty-five years. This despite the fact that Jones had encountered his employer daily in the men's room, the former attending to his business in a literal sense while the latter did the same figuratively. So it came as a surprise when all seventy-six of us received with our paychecks an invitation to a company party at the ballroom of the Presidential Hotel.

As you know, I am not accustomed to attending parties. There are few things that I endure with less gusto than parties. In fact, faced with the choice between a medical exam by an overly zealous proctologist and going to a party, I would unhesitatingly choose the exam. But, as I had pinned my career hopes on one day obtaining the position of CFO of Schmeltzer Industries, I returned my RSVP and steeled myself for the ordeal.

My worst fears were realized. In the center of the ballroom

was a long table holding a faux crystal bowl from the edge of which depended a circle of wan, previously-frozen crustaceans. Next to this were plates of out-of-season fruits, supermarket cheeses, and fuzzy toothpicks. Beside this scene of gastronomic horror stood a forlorn mass of humanity, grasping plastic cups and paper napkins, hoping to avoid meaningful conversation at all costs.

I was reckoning the possibilities of a graceful escape when I heard myself being summoned. "Warren," said the voice of the Younger Mr. Schmeltzer. "There is someone I want you to meet."

My youthful employer was standing beside a middle-aged woman of immense proportions, both vertical and horizontal, with a markedly equine countenance. "This is my Mom, Ruth Schmeltzer," he said displaying filial pride. "Mom, this is Warren Borman, one of our best men in Purchasing."

"Accounting," I corrected him.

"Cool," he said.

The woman was looking at me rapturously through several layers of mascara. "You look like a man who appreciates a good home cooked meal," she said in a husky voice. She took one heavily bejeweled hand and began rubbing my mid-section in a circular motion.

I was dumbstruck. It was the first time my abdomen had been in contact with a female since tripping over a kneeling cheerleader in the eighth grade.

"Why don't you come over to my place for dinner tomorrow night, Warren," she said, inclining her magenta lips toward my ear. Then, winking, she grabbed hold of my trousers and yanked them so forcefully I experienced an intense abrasion across my perineum.

"He'll be there at eight," said the Younger Mr. Schmeltzer.

* * *

The next day around one p.m. the phone rang, rousing me from my usual Sunday hours of repose.

"Warren, this is Mr. Schmeltzer. I was calling to remind you that Mom is expecting you at eight o'clock."

"Yes, sir."

"I wouldn't want you to forget."

"The appointment hasn't left my mind for a moment," I said, rather too truthfully.

"Good. These past few months have been a real drag for Mom. I wouldn't want anyone to let her down. She would be bummed if anyone let her down."

"Yes, sir."

"And I would be bummed if anyone let her down."

"I can only imagine, Mr. Schmeltzer."

"Well, I'm glad we've had a chance to shoot the breeze a little, Warren. You seem like a pretty cool dude."

"To the point of nearly being cold," I said.

* * *

With my career in the balance, I arrived at the Waldorf Arms Apartments precisely at eight. As luck would have it, I had passed a wedding party exiting a nearby church and was able to nip in and pinch several long-stem lilies from the altar.

"I'm here to see Mrs. Schmeltzer," I said to the doorman, a slight fellow with a Hitlerian mustache.

He narrowed his eyes. "Mrs. Ruth Schmeltzer?"

"The very one," I replied.

He took notice of the flowers in my hand. "You taking those to her?"

I assured him that was my sole intention for the bouquet.

"You got a date with her?"

I was becoming irritated at this inquisition. "If you must know, sir, I am dining in with the lady."

What he said next was under his breath, a consideration for which I was grateful. He allowed me to enter and pressed the call button. "Somebody in a mismatched suit here to see you, Mrs. Schmeltzer," he said, as if she were an unfortunate homeowner and he a termite inspector. "Says he's your date."

"Send him up, Ralph," came a dark voice through the speaker.

And up I indeed went.

I had no need to knock on her door as she was waiting for me at the threshold. It was not so much her gold lamé dress, cut low enough to reveal the majority of her prodigious bosoms that made me shudder. It was her substantial forefinger, protruding and bending in a come-hither gesture. "Come in, Warren," she said. "Don't be afraid."

I did, but I was.

The apartment appeared as large as a person of Mrs.

Schmeltzer's dimensions required. I was not able to see much of it, however, because she seemed to have forgotten to turn up the lights. When I pointed this out to her, she only laughed — rather like a panther clearing its throat.

"Sit down and have a drink, Warren." She indicated a long leather couch, draped in shadows of a scented candle. "I'm going to slip into something more comfortable."

It so happened that my knees were beginning to buckle, so I did as I was bid. On the glass coffee table were a crystal goblet and a bottle containing what I made out to be banana brandy. I poured myself a generous helping and sloshed it down, hoping it would take the edge off my anxiety. The position of CFO, I repeated to myself, paid nearly thirty-nine thousand dollars a year.

The silence of my meditation was broken by the sounds of a crooning voice that I was able to identify as that of the late Barry White accompanied by the Love Unlimited Orchestra. I downed another drink.

In a few minutes, my date returned to the room. Mrs. Schmeltzer wore what appeared to be a loose gray sweat suit and red high-topped sneakers. I'm not certain, because at that moment the room began to spin, and my date seemed to be at the end of a very long, dark tunnel. Oddly, the tunnel grew narrower around her face, which was grinning like a thoroughbred who had just won the Kentucky Derby. Then all went black.

* * *

I woke up with a torturous throbbing in my skull. My

first thought was that I had been roundly beaten with a rubber mallet. When I aroused myself I discovered I was still lying on the couch in the Schmeltzer penthouse apartment. Light was pouring in through the curtains. The blue wicker clock on the wall read twenty minutes past ten. I sprang to my feet only to totter backwards.

"Mrs. Schmeltzer?" I whined, holding my throbbing head.

There was no answer.

In fact, there was no one in the entire expanse of apartment. After walking around aimlessly searching for some clue to what had transpired, I left, locking the door behind me.

"So it's you," said Ralph the Doorman as I attempted to make a discreet exit from the lobby. I assured him that I was truly me.

"You just leaving?"

I wanted to say that it was not one moment too soon, but I held my tongue. I had no desire to discuss the vicissitudes of my love life with the public.

* * *

I went straight to work, not taking the time to return to my own apartment. There was a large yellow piece of paper taped to my computer, commanding me to report to the Younger Mr. Schmeltzer immediately upon my arrival. I was disheveled from sleeping in my clothes. I hadn't eaten in nearly twenty-four hours. My face was unshaven and my teeth unbrushed. But I hoisted myself upstairs to the president's office.

"Kind of late, Warren," he said, putting the tips of his fingers together and rotating them.

"Please forgive me, sir," I said to the whelp. "It won't happen again. You may dock me for the entire day if you like."

"The entire day? Ha! That's a laugh." There was something unsettling in his tone. "You spent last night in Mom's apartment."

I was at a loss to respond.

"Don't play games with me, Warren. I know all."

I brightened. "You do, sir? Then perhaps you can explain it to me."

He stood up. "I'll explain it to you, Warren. You took advantage of a dinner invitation from a lonely, vulnerable widow and turned it into an opportunity to get laid. I'll admit that Mom's a hottie, but that's no excuse for satisfying your disgusting cravings by hopping her bones. They've invented a term just for guys like you, Warren. It begins with 'mother' and ends with 'fucker.' Now get out of here. You're fired."

"But, Mr. Schmeltzer—"

He slammed his fist on the intercom button. "Maureen, get Jedediah in here right away. I have a piece of garbage I need removed."

* * *

To say I was distraught would be an understatement. My career hopes appeared dashed forever, made all the more bitter because I hadn't done a thing to deserve it. I cleared out my desk like one in a trance, bade farewell to the boys in the break room, and left the dirty white stucco offices of Schmeltzer Industries for the last time.

For hours I wandered the city, horrified by the specter raised by HELP WANTED signs in windows of greasy spoon restaurants. By nightfall I had stirred myself to such a degree of self-righteous indignation that I my steps irresistibly led me to the grand entrance of the Waldorf Arms Apartments.

The doorman was not to be seen, but I slipped in behind a snow-capped octogenarian with a key. In a trice I was pounding on Mrs. Schmeltzer's penthouse door.

She opened it a crack. "Oh, it's you," she said.

"Enough of 'it's you,'" I said, "and more of what-in-the-name-of-Hades is going on. First you extend an invitation to dine and instead slip me what is colloquially called a 'mickey.' Then your son tosses me out on the sidewalk. What I want to know is why?"

She sniggered. "You've been a pawn, Warren. I was in love with a man but couldn't get him to make a move. I figured if he knew there was another man making time with me, he might get jealous enough to do something about it. And I was right. He did."

I was outraged. "But why? Who—?

"Ruth, dear," came a voice from within. "Are you coming back to bed?"

"Right away, Ralphie," she said.

I pushed the door open far enough to see the doorman, clad in nothing but his cap and an expression of delight, readied for love.

* * *

"A month later," Warren says to the man in the North Face jacket, "I received a wedding invitation from the happy couple. Along with it was a classified advertisement for the position of doorman at the Waldorf Arms Apartments. I responded to neither."

The man in the Northface jacket leans back into the booth. "And you're telling me that's who we just saw in the limo? The mother of your old boss and her husband, the doorman? That story sounds pretty fishy to me."

Warren just smiles, pats the corner of his mouth with his napkin, and picks up the check from the edge of the table. "I believe this is yours," he says.

Turn On, Tune In

"Don't stand there in the rain." The young woman with the long legs reaches across the leather seat of her Toyota Avalon to open the passenger door for the older, slightly stout, slightly balding man with an umbrella. "Get in, Warren," she says.

Warren drops into the seat and shakes his bent umbrella before closing the door. "Thank you for your kind offer," he says.

"Sure. I know you usually take the bus home from work, but I hated to see you waiting in this weather." She uses a finely manicured hand to switch on the wipers and the radio.

A pained expression comes across Warren's face. "Would you mind if I asked you to turn that off?"

"The radio? You don't like that song?"

"It isn't the song, although I hardly classify that puerile whining as a song. It's radio I can't tolerate. I never listen to the radio."

She pauses the car. "Jesus, Warren. You really *are* strange. I've never heard of anybody who was too stuck-up to listen to the radio."

"It's not pride," he says, wiping his wet glasses on his sleeve. "It's simply bitterness, all due to the perfidy of pulchritudinous sirens like yourself."

"Huh?"

"It so happens, my dear, that I have some dry cleaning waiting for me at a small establishment in Kensington. If you would be so kind as to drive all the way up there before you take me home, I will take the opportunity to share my heart-rending tale."

* * *

I was in the fragrant springtime of my life (says Warren), studying liberal arts at a semi-prestigious university. In my sophomore year I developed an intense interest in the *Ferghana* style of Uzbeki classical music. To help promote public awareness of this sadly overlooked genre, I volunteered to host a radio program on our 50-watt college station. Admittedly, the time slot I was given — between 2 and 3 a.m. on Monday mornings — did not offer ample opportunity to reach a wide audience. Nonetheless, I was overflowing with youthful enthusiasm, and so impressionable that I was considering abandoning my academic goals and pursuing a career in radio.

However, it would be grossly negligent to give you the impression that musicology and mass communication were my only motivations. A certain young lady by the name of Roxanne Skenazy also volunteered at the station. She was the hostess of a two-way talk program entitled *What the Hell's Your Problem?* For an hour every evening she took calls from listeners and gave them practical advice on subjects ranging from good study habits to ways to extract more pleasure from the act of physical love. One evening, on a whim and quite anonymously, I called and confessed to carrying a shameful burden in life, to wit, that a stripe of unwanted hair grew down my back. In a voice full of sympathy, she said that in the game of life a little foliage on odd parts of the body wasn't any sort of disqualifier, and I should strive to like myself the way I was.

Never in my wildest speculations had this simple concept occurred to me. I instantly fell in desperate love with this dulcet angel whom I judged a combination of Florence Nightingale and Sigmund Freud. Shortly thereafter I applied for, and was accepted by, the university radio station.

However, being a young man of reserved and studious habits, I had little hope of competing with coarse upperclassmen who flaunted unhygienic grooming and faux criminal personas. Still the fire burned deeply in my bosom.

So you can understand how I was taken aback when she threw open the door of my dorm room one afternoon, making her entrance while I was in the process of applying acne medicine to the inside of my thighs.

"Hey, Warren," she said, apparently unperturbed

that I was crouching bowlegged and wearing nothing but severely unwashed jockey shorts. "How's tricks?"

I flushed with embarrassment and grabbed for my bedspread.

She flopped down on the now exposed sheets of my bed. "I was up late studying on Sunday night and caught your show."

"You did?"

"Yeah, I thought it was far out."

"You did?"

"Yep. I especially liked one song. I can't remember the name but it was real groovy.

"Jurabeg Nabiev's *Gidjak?*"

"That must have been it. A real toe tapper."

In the style of the day she wore a long skirt made from patched blue jeans, broken flip-flop sandals, and a loose sweatshirt with a comic rendering of Albert Einstein across her bra-less chest. My heart was aflame. "Very few people today, "I said, my eyes roaming over a stray bit of ankle, "have an appreciation for the plucked-string dotar."

"Well, you're looking at one chick who does. You know, Warren, I've been asking around about you."

"You have?"

"People say you're a cool guy."

"Which people?"

"Well...just about everyone on campus. They all say you're really hip."

"They do?"

"Yeah. There's a dude I know in your Western Phil class who says you're a whiz at expressing your opinions."

It was true. The child became the father to the man.

She casually pulled her skirt, revealing more of the lower part of a leg unshaven since puberty. "I'd just love to get to know you better, if you know what I mean."

I didn't, but I was frantically trying to guess. "I have nothing on my schedule this afternoon," I said with a sudden swell of expectancy.

"That would be cool, Warren, but I'm afraid it'll have to wait. You see, I'm leaving to go to D.C. for a Militant Feminists for Peace rally. That's what I wanted to talk to you about. I won't be able to do my radio show next week, and I was wondering if you would mind filling in for me."

"Me?"

"You bet. You have just the sort of street-wise attitude that can help people."

I was completely nonplussed. Up to that point I had assumed my street wisdom was limited to my knowledge of the chemical composition of asphalt. "I never looked at it like that before," I said. "But I am very good at discerning the failings of others."

"Of course you are, Warren. That's why I want you for the job. If you do a good job — which I know you will — I'll be really grateful when I get back. I mean really grateful, if you catch my drift."

I caught it.

* * *

Knowing that most professional announcers create an on-the-air persona, I decided to adopt a sobriquet derived from the protagonist of a book I was then writing — an historical novel about a disfigured Peloponnesian cobbler who attempts to introduce the decimal point into the Roman numeral system.

"Is this Xerxes?" asked my first caller.

"It is indeed I," I said. "What the hell's your problem?"

"It's my roommate. He's a real slob. Leaves his dirty clothes all over the dorm room. So far I haven't had the nerve to tell him how much it bothers me. Do you think I should be honest with him and ask him to try to be a little neater?"

I didn't need to think this one over. "Of course not. That sort of verbal approach usually yields little. I find most people simply refuse to entertain negative ideas about themselves. Actions speak much louder than words. Go out and purchase several containers of Rit dye. Number 12 fuchsia would be an excellent choice. When your roommate is absent, gather up as many articles of his wardrobe as possible, take them to the laundry room and wash them in hot water and dye. It will be an object lesson your roommate will not soon forget."

There was a prolonged silence on the other end. I could tell he was impressed. "Are you sure, Mr. Xerxes? That seems pretty drastic."

"If you want lesser advice, go somewhere else."

Suddenly my ears were met with a dial tone. The caller was probably already on his way to the fabric store.

This, I decided, was going to be easier than I thought.

* * *

It was toward the end of the hour when I received her call. She identified herself simply as Molly. There was an undercurrent of desperation in her young voice, and I knew at once it was imperative that I dispense the best possible advice.

"It's my boyfriend," she said. "I really, really love him, but lately he's been pressuring me to go farther with him — physically, I mean — farther than I feel comfortable. Do you think I should tell him how much I love him and ask him to wait until I'm ready?"

I took a deep breath and thought hard. "Bengay, my dear.

"What?"

"The popular over-the-counter unguent. Apply it liberally, not neglecting intimate areas."

"But...but doesn't that stink?"

I was astounded at the woman's obtuseness. "That is precisely the point."

"But...I don't understand how that will help."

I wasn't able to conceal a light laugh. "I've given you advice. Whether you take it or not is up to you. But it's the future of *your* romance at stake, not mine."

"Well, if you really think—"

"I do."

* * *

The next night Molly called back. "Things didn't work out very well, Xerxes," she said. "I used the Bengay like you told me. My boyfriend said it really turned him on. It reminded him of when he played football in high school. I had to struggle to keep him from grabbing my blouse in the delicatessen. By the time he took me home, he was pretty mad. He said he thought I was a tease. I really don't want to lose him, Mr. Xerxes. What should I do?"

I scratched my chin, a gesture that was of course wasted on her. "If we aren't able to dissuade him physically," I said finally, "then we must use psychology. Fortunately there are fewer things in the universe more fragile than the male ego. I advise you to invite him to your dormitory for what you promise will be a memorable evening. Have the lights lowered and romantic music playing. One of the Barrys is preferable — Manilow or White, it makes little difference. After our subject arrives, invite him to undress in front of you. When he does, which he surely will, laugh uncontrollably at his anatomy. The laughter of a woman when confronted by a man's most prized feature has the same effect as a fire extinguisher does to a match."

* * *

The following day I found a picture postcard in my letterbox. It was the image of the Statue of Liberty holding not a torch but a burning bra. On the reverse were these words in a delicate female hand: *Dear Warren, I just know you're doing an out of sight job on the show. I have every confidence in you. You are so groovy. Just remember to be yourself. Affectionately yours, Roxy.*

Be myself! Another astounding suggestion. Once again I was filled with a rush of emotion that went far beyond admiration. I took the postcard, tied it up in lavender ribbon and placed in under my pillow.

* * *

"Mr. Xerxes, this is Molly again. I did just what you told me to do."

"Wonderful, my dear. I hope the two of you now will be very happy."

"You don't understand. I had him take off his pants. When I started to laugh, he did, too. He said he liked a woman who had a good sense of humor. Then he asked me to take off my clothes. I didn't know what to do. He finally stormed out, telling me he couldn't stand much more of my teasing. I'm so afraid of losing him. I think I should just give in. Maybe it would be all right after all."

A picture of Roxanne lying prone across my bed flashed through my mind, enhanced slightly by my colorful imagination. I was determined to solve this poor young woman's problem. Drastic action, I realized, was called for.

"My dear Molly. If you compromise your principles now, this man will never respect you. You must assert the rights to your personal boundaries. There only one course left open. I recommend you purchase a small handgun, possibly an American Derringer stainless steel Remington standard Model 1. Keep it handy at all times.

Tuck it into the garter of your stockings if you wear them. When your boyfriend makes an unwanted advance, produce the firearm and explain your position to him clearly and in words impossible to misinterpret. I assure you that he will apprehend your message."

"I don't think I can do that, Xerxes," she said after a significant pause. "It just doesn't seem right to pull a gun on the man I love."

"Right?" I was amazed by her lack of courage. "Is it right that you have been put into this untenable position? If I were you, this situation would have been rectified long ago. For goodness sake, woman, summon some fortitude and do your duty."

"I...I don't know," she stammered.

"Well, I do," I said firmly.

* * *

"Who is this?" I inquired into the microphone the next evening. "Speak plainly. I can't understand you."

"It's Molly," sobbed a weak voice. "Something awful has happened."

I felt a wave of impatience, but I held my emotions in check. After all, I was a public servant. "What is it now, my dear?"

"I...I don't know how to tell you this, Mr. Xerxes. I bought a gun like you told me to. When my boyfriend put his arm around me and tried to unbutton my blouse, I...I took it out and was going to...to make my point, just like you said. But I had never used a gun before. I thought they had safety locks on them or something."

"Oh, dear."

"I never felt so horrible in my life. I realized that I had shot the only man I had ever loved."

"Is he…how is he…?" I asked, fearing the worst.

"I just grazed his foot," she said, gasping. "He's going to be fine. It's me that's gotten the worst of it. The dorm captain called the police when she heard the shot. They came and were going to charge me with assault with a deadly weapon, but the president of the university bailed me out. He said he had no choice but to order my immediate expulsion from school. I'm packing my things and heading back to Iowa." There was a brief interlude of tears and choking. "C-can you help me?"

This was truly an unforeseen development. I simply couldn't fathom how my foolproof plan could have gone awry.

"I confess I'm out of suggestions," I said to her, "other than to remind you there is excellent train service out of Pittsburgh."

* * *

Saturday dawned cold and dreary. I was sick to my stomach. I had literally ruined someone's life. Worse than that, I had let down Roxanne. She had entrusted the collective soul of the university to my care. I lay in dread of the confession I was obliged to make.

The inevitable moment came. Roxanne came bounding into my room about 11 a.m. "Just came by to offer you my undying gratitude, Warren," she beamed.

"I don't deserve it." I lowered my eyes to the floor, a rather disturbing action as I was not as fastidious as I am today. "I...I let you down, Roxanne."

"Let me down? Of course you didn't."

"Oh, I did. You told me to be myself. I'm afraid that self was woefully inadequate to dispense personal advice. I was instrumental in having an innocent young woman expelled from the university."

She smiled with what I first took to be a smile of forgiveness and encouragement. I was wrong.

"Ah, the case of Molly. You don't understand, Warren. You did just what I knew you would. For months I've had a terrible crush on Molly's boyfriend, Scabby. I just haven't been able to figure out a way to get her out of the picture. I knew before I went away she wanted some advice about their relationship. I kindly gave her a tip to call in my radio show, but only after I arranged for somebody to take my place who was sure to fuck things up royally. That somebody was you."

I was appalled. The curtain fell from my eyes. I realized that what I had taken for love was simply the ignorant infatuation of a naive schoolboy. And whom I had taken for an angel was, in fact, a devil in a tie-dyed midi-blouse.

"B-but what was all that about showing my your gratitude when you got back?"

"Oh, yeah. I almost forgot." She reached into her macramé handbag and fished out a worn paper bag. "For you," she said. "It's a rock that somebody threw at a cop.

Hit him square on the helmet. I managed to find it and save it. Bound to be an historic relic."

* * *

"It was about three years ago," Warren says to the young woman driving the Avalon, "that I received an unexpected letter postmarked Des Moines. It was a thank you note from Molly. She had used the Internet to locate Roxanne from whom she obtained my real name. She wanted me to know that getting away from college and Scabby was the best thing that ever happened to her. She eventually went to nursing school, met and married a handsome doctor and, at the time of her writing me, had three nearly grown children, the oldest of which she had named Xerxes. The happy couple was planning to take an early retirement to a small Caribbean island they had purchased with their spare change. Roxanne it seems, after a brief residence in the California State Penitentiary, became the host of an all-night neo-conservative radio program in San Jose."

"Oh, come on, Warren," she says, adjusting the speed of her windshield wipers. "You didn't really get a girl thrown out of college by telling her to pull a gun on her boyfriend. I don't believe that."

Warren smiles. "There's my dry cleaner up ahead. I confess I forgot that I must make a brief stop at my bank. Unfortunately, it's all the way back downtown. I'm sure you won't mind."

Political Camp Pains

"He's the sort of guy who wouldn't give his grandma a bent nickel if she were begging on the street. He's got to be a Republican." The bearded man wearing a black NO FEAR tee shirt is talking loud enough to be overheard by the subject of his remark — a slightly older, slightly stouter, and slightly balder man sitting by himself at the other end of the otherwise empty bar.

A man in a blue serge suit shakes his head. "Warren Borman? That effete intellectual? He has to be a Democrat."

"You're both wrong," says a thin man in crew neck sweater. "I've heard him rant about the government. I'd be willing to bet he's a Libertarian."

"Oh, yeah?" says the bearded man. "A twenty says he's a Republican."

"I'm in," says the man in the blue serge suit, reaching into his breast pocket. "My twenty says Democrat. Gertz, you in? Winner take all."

Warren puts down his glass of Merlot. "Did I hear you gentlemen say something about a bet?"

"We only meant—"

"I know exactly what you meant," says Warren. "You three have nothing better to do than attempt to violate the sanctity of the American voting booth by provoking me into revealing my political allegiance."

"We wouldn't—," begins the man in the blue serge suit.

"Of course you would," says Warren. "And even though you have no right to hear it, I will tell you the remarkable story of my experience in politics, as you have decided to turn it into a wager.

"We don't have much ...," says the man in the crew neck sweater.

"Certainly you do. Sixty dollars is at stake. Just put your money down there on the table."

* * *

Having graduated from college (says Warren), I obtained an entry-level position in a firm in a southern state that shall remain nameless. My co-workers, in true loyalty to their local economy, smoked incessantly. I often sought refuge from my polluted cubicle in a small, shaded picnic area behind the building. That is where I first saw her.

She was breathtaking. Her curly locks were the color of a five-year-old penny, and the freckles on her face, arms, and legs lent her the ethereal beauty of Seurat painting.

"Hey," she said in a southern drawl that quite stole my breath. "You're new around here."

"Warren Borman," I said, extending a hand trembling from the sudden onset of emotion. "And you are correct. I have lived here only a few weeks."

"Are you registered?" I must have displayed bafflement because she leaned closer to explain. "Your voter registration. Are you registered to vote in the upcoming election?"

Like most educated Americans, I had been taught the basics of a democratic government. However, as politics — taking a back seat only to religion — was considered an unsuitable subject for conversation, I wasn't aware of ever knowing anyone who actually voted.

"We're in the middle of the most critical gubernatorial race in a century," she said. "For the last six years we've been under the rule of a fascist reactionary Republican named Fred Smellman. Our only hope of returning justice to this state is the Democratic candidate, State Representative Jack Rankin. Here you go." She said, reaching her speckled arm deep into her substantial purse. "I'm not allowed to politic at work, but since we're technically not working, I can give you these." She produced — in this order — a Rankin button, a Rankin bumper sticker, a rolled Rankin poster, and a Rankin rally flyer.

"The rally's Friday evening after work. I could come by your office and we could go together. That way we could get to know each other better." She twirled her red polka dotted skirt in a typically southern coquettish fashion.

Everything seemed to be quickening, including my pulse. "B...but, I don't know your name."

"Linda," she said. "Linda Lovelace."

Or that is what I shall call her.

* * *

The rally turned out to be less than the stellar event I had been anticipating. The majority of supporters of Democratic Representative Jack Rankin wore their hair long — the male version being tucked in gaudy headbands, the female ironed to resemble drapery. A barefoot fellow with kaleidoscopic sunglasses stood gaping at my stylish checked polyester suit. "Hey, man," he said. "You look like The Man."

I stood pondering this cryptic statement, wondering if manners required me to thank him, until Linda took my arm and led me through the throng up to a large pig-tailed blonde who at first glance I took for a lead soprano in a Wagnerian opera. All that was missing was a horned helmet.

"Warren, I'd like you to meet Val Odorly," said Linda. "She's Jack Rankin's campaign manager."

"Glad to have you on board," she said, shaking my hand so vigorously I worried for the springs in my self-winding watch. She grabbed my lapel and ran her eyes up the entire length of my body. "Listen, why don't the two of you join me after the speech for a little chow-down?"

Linda clasped her hands. "Ooh, how exciting! Isn't that exciting, Warren?"

Before I could formulate a reply, the candidate took the stage. One look and I wondered if Linda had been rash in pinning her hopes on such a prospect. Jack Rankin was slight with a weak chin and voluminous bags under his eyes. A less likely looking politician — even in the South — I couldn't imagine. However, after clearing his throat several times, Rankin delivered a marvelous speech. He spoke quietly yet persuasively about government's responsibilities to the underprivileged and the deprived and so forth and so on. I confess I was quite moved.

And thus within the hour I found myself sitting with Linda and Val, the Viking Soprano, at a local restaurant that served an extraordinary dish to which the waitress gave the surprising sobriquet *hush puppies*.

"Jack's really something, isn't he, Warren?" Linda's green eyes were twinkling.

"Something is exactly the word that springs to mind," I said, refraining from bringing up the use of teabags under the eyes as a cosmetic aid.

"Look here, Wally," said Val, throwing a substantial arm around my shoulder. "Frankly...may I speak frankly?"

I assured her that, although my name was Warren, she could.

"We got ourselves a good campaign going, but you know those Republicans."

I didn't, of course.

"Jack's got lots of strong supporters, but they tend to — how do I put it? — all have the same kind of look. What we're in need of is a man who's liberal but looks like he's a conservative — like he's got a two-by-four stuck up his ass. Well, someone like you."

"She means that in the nicest possible way," said Linda.

"Could we count on you, Wally, to help out the campaign in a very special way?"

Prior to that afternoon, I cared little which party was in power or when, but Rankin's speech had brought me cogently into the Democratic fold. That, plus the hand of Linda, which had somehow crept under the tablecloth and was resting provocatively on my knee.

"I'll do it," I said, giving my freckled beauty a sidelong glance and a meaningful wink. "By the way, what am I doing?"

The Viking Soprano produced a plain brown bag. "Tomorrow Governor Smellman will be giving a speech. When it's over, you'll go up to his campaign manager, Sid Putrib, and give him this."

I opened it. My accountant's brain acted with lightning speed. "This is $20,000 in hundred dollar bills."

"You'll give it to him as a contribution to Smellman's campaign."

I doubted both my ears and her sanity. "But...but why...?"

"I know Sid Putrib. Getting that much money in cash will make you his best friend for life. When you tell him you want to volunteer for the campaign, it'll be all you can do to keep him from smothering you with kisses."

"But what…?"

"You'll be in a perfect position to report back to us what's going on in their campaign."

"But how…?"

"Every week you can meet Linda in some quiet, dark spot and pass along the information."

I turned to Linda. A daub of pork barbecue remained on the side of her mouth, perfectly complementing the crimson in her freckles. The word "spy" vanished from my mind. So did "espionage," "deceit," "subterfuge," "dissembling," and "unseemly." So did the memory of an entire semester spent in Ethics class. I was lost in the verdant eyes of my bespotted maiden.

"I'll do it," I said, deftly avoiding the offer of another handshake with the Viking Soprano. "But only to help further the cause of government's responsibilities to the underprivileged and the deprived and so forth and so on."

"There'll be a place in Jack's administration for a young man with your skills. By the way, Wally, what sort of skills do you have?"

* * *

The difference between the two candidates' rallies could not have been more striking. There must have been four hundred other men in identical stylish checkered polyester suits. And then there was governor himself, a hale fellow well-met if I had ever seen one. He was stocky and ruggedly handsome, with a chin dimple in which it looked possible to hide his car keys.

He spoke long and passionately about the natural beauty of the state, its distinctive cuisine, and even the prowess of its university basketball teams — subjects I wasn't quite able to connect to his tenure as head of state. But he had the crowd laughing, crying, and cheering.

When the hysteria abated, I made my way through the sea of supporters until I found Sid Putrib, the governor's campaign manager. He was exactly as described, a wiry man with a face adorned with an pubescent mustache and topped with what looked like a black, oily, corrugated tin roof.

"Mr. Putrib?" He turned to me as if I were a cockroach he had discovered in his raisins. "I'd like the governor to have this," I said, handing him the envelope.

He snatched it from my hand and looked inside. "Jesus fuckin' Christ," he said. "That must be ten grand in cash."

"Twenty," I said, wanting the man to appreciate the full tableau. "To help out the cause, being myself a staunch Republican and desirous of volunteering my time for your candidate's campaign on behalf of the wealthy and privileged."

"Hell, yeah, sonny. For twenty grand you can even sleep with my wife."

I assured him that my ambitions lay in a different arena.

"Good choice," he said, slapping my back.

* * *

Everything proceeded as planned. Sid invited me to join the exclusive Governor's Club, a society of six or eight middle-aged men who seemed more interested in the consumption of alcohol and in wagering on the outcomes of university football games than politics. In fact, the only reference the governor ever made to his campaign was offhand — a disparaging and surprisingly graphic remark about his opponent's wife's breasts.

Yet, the whole escapade was made thrilling by my weekly rendezvous with Linda. For our trysts, she had chosen a small, all-night diner whose proprietors practiced remarkable economy with their electrical lighting.

Over glasses of highly sweetened iced tea and plates of key lime pie, she listened intently to my reports, recording every detail into a small, black notebook. Although the lack of substantive material was a disappointment to her, I was anything but disappointed. Even in the dimness of our rear booth I was entranced by the multitude of brown stars that bedecked her features.

"Please be patient, my dear," I said to her. "Surely something will happen sooner or later."

And sooner it did.

* * *

"War'," said Sid Putrib, placing a perspiring arm around my shoulder the very next night. "I've been talking to The Gov, and he says he'd like to get to know you a little better. Says he thinks you're a smart cookie and might have some good ideas about how to woo the youth vote."

"Actually," I said, escaping the arm, "I've been thinking about how the Governor can explain his tax cuts for the wealthy by a scheme I humorously call 'trickle down' economics."

"Sure, sure, sure. You just save it for The Gov, War'. He'd like you to come by the Executive Mansion tomorrow night, say, about midnight. The front door is locked, so just use The Gov's private entrance. Oh, I almost forgot. There's a few things he'd like you to pick up on the way over."

He proceeded to dictate a shopping list including, as I recall, flour, sugar, butter, eggs, whipping cream, vanilla, maraschino cherries, and two aprons with frilly edges. I was so brightened by the prospect of having a private audience with the governor I never gave consideration to the strangeness of the request. I was much more concerned about bearing the cost of the items, as I was then of some straitened means.

However, I did as bid and at five minutes to twelve the following evening I climbed the stairs of the private entrance to the governor's quarters.

"Mr. Borman — may I call you Warren? — please come in. I see you brought the things I asked for. Well, if we're going to make cupcakes, we'd better get started. But first," he said with a wink, "let's put on our aprons. We wouldn't want to get flour on us, would we?"

And so we did. We spent the better part of the next hour wrapped in pink aprons with frilly edges, sifting flour, melting butter, mixing batter, and finally eating the results of our labor. I waited, patient and eager for an opportunity to broach the subject of politics. "Governor Smellman," I said at last, "I was wondering—"

"Call me Smeckers," he said, offering me a glass of Yoo-Hoo from his refrigerator. "That's what all my close friends call me." And he gave me a smile identical to that on his campaign posters.

I hesitated. "Well...Smeckers, I was wondering—"

He laughed. "Of course. How could I forget? Here's a twenty. That should cover everything. Listen, pal, how about coming back over tomorrow night? Same time. I just need you to pick up a few things."

And of course, I did. It required locating sources for a large galvanized tub, a basket of Macintosh apples and two pirate costumes, one with a plumed hat. Frankly I was unable to see much entertainment in donning comic regalia and placing our heads in a tub of water attempting to bite apples. But the governor displayed unrestrained enthusiasm, getting much enjoyment from imitating a Hollywood version of a cockney accent.

My private evenings with the governor became a series of increasingly bizarre affairs. Of the night with the eight commercial-sized containers of mayonnaise, the bag of chicken feathers, and the jelly beans, I cannot bring myself to speak. Suffice it to say that, although I was not able to bring a report of any political campaign activity, I looked forward with eager anticipation to my next meeting with Linda.

Her reaction did not disappoint me. Her eyes grew to the size of two green china tea saucers. "Unbelievable," she said, finally finding her voice. "I knew Fred Smellman was a right-wing extremist. I didn't know he was mentally unbalanced."

"Only if you consider chasing white mice around a living room with a fondue fork to be mentally unbalanced," I said.

She scribbled faster than I thought humanly possible. "Wait until Val reads this. This should kill Smellman's chances for re-election." She took my hand and brought it to her cheek. "You are so sweet and brave for doing this, Warren."

"I'm just glad to do my part to help the disadvantaged and the deprived and so forth and so on," I said, hoping to hide my blush in the plentiful shadows.

* * *

For the next night, the governor had asked me to meet him in a large commercial building in the downtown area. Brushing past a homeless man who requested I invest in his rehabilitation, I arrived as directed at a fifth floor office carrying a box with that day's requested items. Instead of the governor, I found Sid Putrib lurking in the dark hallway.

"War', The Gov was called away to some important state government-type business," he said, taking the box.

"Said he was real sorry and for you just to leave the stuff with me. I'll get it to him later. Thanks a mil, War'. Just keep the receipt and the Gov will pay you back."

Grateful for the chance to have a night to myself, I shook Sid's hand, immediately wiped mine on my pants, and went home.

I slept quite soundly that night and woke refreshed. But when I opened my door to find the daily newspaper, my sense of well being vanished. I was astounded by the headline article.

PSYCHIATRIST'S RECORDS SHOW
RANKIN A BEDWETTER.

I grabbed the paper and feverishly read the story. A burglar had made forced entrance into the office of a local psychiatrist, stolen the private medical records of the Democratic candidate, and left them anonymously on the doorstep of *The Daily Observer*. The papers revealed that Jack Rankin was under treatment for a number of psychological difficulties, not the least of which was enuresis, a condition that had plagued Rankin since he had returned from serving in Viet Nam.

My first thought was for poor Linda, whose hero now had no chance at all of winning. I knew that Americans in general disapproved of mental illness and that no right-thinking Southern voter would abide a governor who regularly soiled the gubernatorial sheets. I felt quite like weeping and would have, had I not noticed the address of the psychiatrist's office as reported in the article.

It was the very same building, floor and office where I had handed Sid Putrib a box containing a brace and bit, a file, a chisel, and a crowbar. "An amazing coincidence," I was just thinking to myself when the doorbell rang. There were three men in black suits and sunglasses, brandishing small identification cards. "State Bureau of Investigation," one said. "May we come in?"

* * *

"You were set up!" says the man in the crew neck sweater.

"You were a stooge!" says the bearded man in the NO FEAR T-shirt.

"You were framed!" says the man in the blue serge suit.

"Like the Mona Lisa in the Louvre," says Warren, wiping a drop of Merlot from his chin. "It took the agents less than two minutes to locate the receipt for the tools that had been left at the scene of the crime. The homeless man in the street whom I had brushed aside was the star witness. He later became the Republican Party candidate for Secretary of Labor.

"Being, as I said, of straitened means, I was represented by the public defender, a man whose wife was the second cousin of the governor. The counselor assured me if I answered all questions honestly all would come right in the end.

"I did as he advised. When put on the stand, I reported the details of my nights with the governor, or rather with Smeckers, as I had been accustomed to calling him. My testimony only served to amuse the jury who had to be reprimanded numerous times for their rollicking expressions of incredulity."

"Did you tell them you were working for the Democrats?" asks the man in the crew neck sweater.

"Alas, the Democrats denied having any association with me. They, of course, blamed me for sabotaging the election. When Linda testified, she said the only relationship we had was one occasion when I had trod on her foot in the elevator."

"And the Republicans?"

"Sid Putrib told the judge that no Republican would ever stoop so low as to break into a man's private office. Of course, the fact that the judge was the brother-in-law of the step-father of the governor's nephew was not in my favor."

The bearded man shakes his head. "Jeez! What happened to you, Warren?"

"From the beginning of the trial there was no doubt I would be found guilty. However, before I was thrown in jail, my sentence was commuted by the governor who, he said, had extraordinary pity for a man who was obviously insane."

The man in the blue serge suit reaches for the bills on the table. "Well, fellows," he says. "He obviously couldn't be a Republican after that. He admitted he had been swayed to the Democratic Party."

"After the girl he loved denied him in his hour of need? No way he could still be a Democrat," says the bearded man, grabbing the wrist of the man in the blue serge suit.

"I knew he hated both parties," says the man in the crew neck sweater. "I don't blame him for being a Libertarian." He takes hold of the bearded man's arm.

"You gentlemen have overlooked a critical factor," says Warren. "Stealing confidential medical records is a felony. As a convicted felon, I have not been eligible to vote for over thirty years. And since each of you has lost," he says, rising and taking the bills off the table, "the house keeps the kitty."

FOILED AGAIN

When the bus door swings open, a man with a blue umbrella steps inside followed by his companion, a man in a black toggle rain jacket. Behind them both is a slightly shorter, slightly stouter, slightly balder, and considerably wetter man.

"Jesus, what the hell was that all about?" asks the man in the toggle jacket.

The man with the blue umbrella takes a seat, shaking water on the bus floor. "I have no idea. That crazy old crone came out of nowhere and started screaming."

"What was that noise she was making?"

"You got me. It sounded like gibberish. And the way she looked at me — it was freakin' scary."

The slightly shorter, stouter, very wet man behind them clears his throat. "My good friends, I witnessed the entire incident, including some portions you did not observe." The man with the umbrella and the man in the toggle jacket turn their heads in unison.

"What do you mean, Warren?" asks the man with the umbrella.

"That was not a crazy old crone," says Warren. "That was the witch Madame Vladescu. For over forty years she's been the proprietress of Madame Vladescu's Shoppe of Magik. And that was not gibberish she was speaking. It was the dreaded Unspeakable Transylvanian Curse."

The man with the umbrella smiles, then grimaces, then blanches. "The what?" he says trying to regain his smile. There is a small tremble in his voice.

"Madame Vladescu was caught in the unexpected downpour. She tried several times unsuccessfully to get your attention, but you were busy expounding your favorite celebrity's proficiency in the art of ballroom dancing. Madame was merely seeking shelter under your umbrella. After what she considered a series of disrespectful rebuffs, she responded by casting a curse upon you.

"Warren, I...I had no idea. But how do you know...?"

"If you would be so kind as to switch places and allow me to sit down, I will explain my familiarity with Transylvanian magic and perhaps convince you how precarious your situation is."

* * *

As a teen, (says Warren) I possessed a mind that was brilliant beyond my years. Unlike my nominal peers who spent their idle hours testing the bounds of parental limits in the shrubbery of our local park, I looked for ways to satisfy my unquenchable thirst for knowledge. My greatest pleasure was to bicycle downtown to a certain rare and used bookstore and browse for hours through recondite tomes.

One gray and dreary afternoon, immersed in a particularly fascinating treatise, I lost all track of time. By the time the exasperated shopkeeper locked the door behind me, a drizzle was falling from the sky. I prudently tucked my weekly purchase under my shirt, but not so prudently decided to take an unfamiliar short cut home. I soon became disoriented in a honeycomb of darkened one-way streets. A misguided hunch brought me to an alley where a forlorn wind whistled through gaping windows of abandoned tenements.

There, in the middle of the block, like a lone living cell in a decaying body, was Madame Vladescu's Shoppe of Magik. It was not only the rumble of approaching thunder that made me bring my bicycle to a halt under her tattered awning. Nor was it the fact I had just purchased a well-worn copy of *Dreadful Folklore of Transylvania* that seized my attention. It was a small sign in the lighted window:

INFLAME HER PASSION WITH
JOHN THE CONQUEROO LOVE CHARM.

You see, I was in those days in the grip of a feverish, unrequited love for a certain pigtailed young lady named Agatha Winfelder. She sat in front of me in biology class; her strawberry blonde braids dangling across the back of her chair. Being a youth through whom the red corpuscles raged as fiercely as any other, I had developed a vivid fantasy life involving the two of us that startled even me. Unfortunately Agatha did not return my advances.

I had done everything a youth could do to win her affections. I found her well-chewed pencil on the floor and left it on her desk while her attention was directed elsewhere. I confided my infatuation to my closest male comrades. I even went so far as to write her name in large letters on my three-ring binder. None of these things seemed to have helped advance my wooing. I was stymied.

Could I be blamed for turning to the occult?

That stormy night when I pushed open the door of Madame Vladescu's Shoppe of Magik, the proprietress did not look up from the large puce crystal that sat in front of her on the back counter. Even then she appeared to be a woman of great age, her eyes nearly covered by a patched shawl, her neck swaddled in gold. Over her left shoulder was draped the fur of some unfortunate creature into whose eye sockets a taxidermist with a flair for the dramatic had placed blood-red rubies.

I swallowed the lump rising in my throat and asked, "Would you be so kind as to tell me where I might find your John the Conqueroos?"

She did not raise her head, but merely indicated a direction with a long finger terminating in a stiletto of a nail. I followed her direction to a draped wooden box on a rickety table. Removing the cover I saw what appeared to be a coiled mass of petrified fetal rodents. They were in fact, a collection of grotesque roots. But far more grotesque to me was the small sign crudely taped to the box: $20. EACH.

I did not have twenty dollars. Truth be told, I barely had twenty cents, having spent my little all at the bookstore, "Put the thought out of your mind, Warren," whispered the stern voice of my conscience. "Take your hand away. No, don't pick one up. What are you doing? Are you crazy?"

But I was crazy. Crazy with love for Agatha Winfelder. Just the feeling of the gnarled texture of the talisman filled me with a current of vigor I had never before known. I went to slip it into my pants pocket, stealing in addition a quick glance in the direction of the Madame. It was during that second, that mere fraction of a second, that a burst of lightning shattered the darkness of the store. In its glare, time froze, revealing in horrific detail both the act of my theft and the fearsome countenance of Madame Vladescu, her glowing green eyes fixed upon me.

"Schtttopp!" she screamed. There was something in her voice — that hideous voice — that momentarily left me unable to move my limbs.

But the power of the talisman had given me access to a hitherto untapped source of inner strength. Once the charm contacted my hip, I felt energy rise inside my P.F. Flyers. I bounded toward the door.

"*Bistrita brasov cluj napoca!*" cackled the voice behind me. "*Medias sebes!*" I could feel the hot breath of the sorceress even though twenty feet separated her lips from my ear. *"Sibiu sighisoara!"* I nearly dislodged the door-knob as I flung myself into the tempest of the night and on the seat of my trusty two-wheeled steed.

How I made it home I have no recollection. Nevertheless I arrived, drenched to my skin and, after consuming two warm bowls of Chef Boyardee Spaghetti-Os, went straight to my room. I took the Conqueroo, no worse for the journey, and tucked it safely in the top drawer of my dresser.

I felt an uncharacteristic rush of manly victory. Having been blessed with gifts of the mind rather than the flesh, I had never experienced the satisfaction of scoring a field goal, hitting a home run, or punching a weaker boy in the face. I had mustered the fortitude to attempt and achieve something bold, daring — some-thing possibly a minor felony. I preened myself in the dresser mirror, exquisitely virile, powerful, and invulnerable.

Or was I?

No matter how strongly I tried to force the strange words of Madame Vladescu from my consciousness, they continued to insinuate their way back. I showered. I put on my pajamas. I climbed into bed, but I could not silence the cackly voice echoing in my mind.

After an hour of tossing and another of turning, I switched on the light and began to peruse my newly purchased copy of *Dreadful Folklore of Transylvania.* I found it on page 427, under the disturbing listing: Catastrophically Evil Curses.

"Bistrita brasov cluj napoca. Medias sebes. Sibiu sighi-soara — *thus are the words of the Unspeakable Transylvanian Curse, bringing gruesome consequences upon the heads of its wretched victims. (See also:* 'Horrific Fates' *p.313 and* 'Worst Things You Can Possibly Imagine' *p.666)*"

I laughed aloud at the ignorance of superstitious peas-antry who could possibly have fallen for such obvious tripe in the 17th century. I was a post-war American youth living in a middle-class suburb, proud of his intel-lectual heritage. I chucked the book into a pile of dirty clothes, leapt out of bed, and yanked open my dresser drawer. There was John the Conqueroo in all his mori-bund splendor, ready to sweep Agatha Winfelder off her patent-leather shoes. There was the fate of my love life, the attainment of my romantic dreams, the achievement of my manhood. What were a few foreign words uttered by an angry shopkeeper compared to the firm, throbbing resolve I felt coursing through my veins?

When the first rays of dawn slipped between my vene-tian blinds, I was ready to conquer, if not the world, at least the heart of Agatha Winfelder. After a thorough practice shave and, to my mother's surprise, a breakfast of oysters, I mounted my bike, John the Conqueroo emanating his power from the left breast pocket of my jacket.

I reached the park in record time. Agatha was on a bench near the bushes, chattering with her clutch of giggling females. I strode toward them, each step a better imitation of John Wayne than the last.

"Oh, hello, Warren," she said. There was a strange light in her eyes. "Funny, we were just talking about you." A whisper of poorly suppressed laughter rippled through our audience.

"Hello, Agatha." I touched my breast pocket for a quick reinforcement of courage. "There's...there's something I want to say to you."

"Cool. There's something I want to say to you, too, Warren."

"You do? I mean, there is?"

"Yeah, why don't we just step over here?"

"Huh?"

I wasn't sure what happened next. She stood, took a step toward me, I took a step back, she put out her hands, and the next thing I knew we were both behind the shrubbery on our knees. "Kiss me, Warren," she said.

"But Agatha—"

"You must know how hot you are, Warren. Can you blame a poor girl for falling under your spell?"

Whether or not these words preceded an escape of girlish laughter from the bench out of sight, I will never know. All I remember is that Agatha lunged at me like a tigress upon a piece of flank steak. I retreated, but a phalanx of boxwood branches held me fast.

"Kiss me, you big strong hunk of man."

"Ah...ah...ah." I tried to speak, to reason with her if possible, and if not, to summon help, but no words would come. My jaw muscles were paralyzed. She came closer. I could smell the Dentyne on her breath. "Ah..ah.. ah." It was as if I had been made mute.

Was I afraid of a mere schoolgirl? I refused to believe that a man as powerful as me could be so weak.

Then it hit me.

It must have been the Curse — and I, its victim who could not speak. That was why it was called Unspeakable. I was flooded with an unbearable vision of a wasted lifetime, struck dumb, unable to share my many gifts with the world.

I broke free of Agatha's surprisingly strong clasp and plunged through the prison of underbrush. I ignored the brambles and the cruel peal of Agatha's giggling and I raced back to my bike. In a trice I traced my path back to Madame Vladescu's Shoppe of Magik. The witch was exactly where she had been the previous night, staring into her magic sphere. "Here you are, miserable woman," I cried from the door. "Take back your wretched talisman!" I threw it at her. She reached up and caught the damnable object without taking her eye from the crystal.

I hardly noticed her athletic prowess. I was too relieved to have recovered my voice. The curse had been lifted.

* * *

"Wow," says the man in the black toggle rain jacket. "That's some story."

The man with the blue umbrella shakes his head, takes a deep breath, and releases it audibly. "Wh..wh…" he begins.

"Oh, dear," says Warren. "I'm afraid the curse is beginning to work. There's only one way to lift it. You must give your umbrella to Madame Vladescu. Do you know where to find her? No, don't try to speak. It will only make matters worse. Here, this is my stop. Give the umbrella to me and I'll make sure she gets it. Don't worry. It will stop raining soon, I'm certain. At least moderately certain."

THE GREAT LINGERIE STAKES

"Simply put, I consider office gambling to be morally reprehensible."

The expectant smile disappears from the face of the young man with the blue tie and tan Dockers. "Geez, Mr. Borman," he says. "It's just a football pool. I didn't know you were so religious."

Warren Borman, slightly older, slightly stouter, and slightly balder, swivels in his chair to hide his computer monitor. "I am not referring to religious morals," he says. "I earned an understanding of the perils of office gambling through bitter experience. I will offer you the benefit of my wisdom if you will, in turn, do me a small favor."

"A favor? What kind of favor?"

"A very small one. One that will be worth more than what it costs, I assure you."

The young man in the Dockers scratches at his collar. "I don't know, Mr. Borman."

"Here, take my chair. No, don't sit where you can see my computer. It will only distract you."

"But, Mr. Borman, I have to—"

"Yes," says Warren, placing a firm hand on the young man's shoulder. "I'm sure you do."

* * *

It began on a fine fall afternoon, one remarkably like this (says Warren). I was then in the employment of Fuerst Quality Products and, in following my daily routine, was in the company break room seeking respite from the onerous tedium of severe underemployment.

I was immersed in the current issue of *Travel and Leisure*, savoring my imported baklava when the solitude was broken by the entrance of a rowdy group of engineers from Research and Development. The central figure in this rabble was Craig Fitzsimmons, a thick-necked fellow who was in the merciless habit of flooding my email box with crude solicitations for weight-loss and hair-weave products. His shirtsleeves were rolled to his upper arms; he clutched a clipboard and a thick stack of bills.

"Okay, animals, hold it down," he said. "Today's winner is McCabe who had $100 on *red tube top, navy skirt, and red sling-back pumps* at ten to one." Stiles had $75 on *blue skirt and red shoes* to place. Too bad, Harding. You should have known she spilled raspberry yogurt on her white V-neck last week." He peeled off several bills and passed them over to the grasping hands of the lucky pair.

"What the devil are you up to, Fitzsimmons?" I asked, slipping the baklava under my magazine.

He looked up from his clipboard. "Didn't see you there, Borman. Just a bit of harmless office fun."

"What's all this about tubes and pumps?"

He grinned like a child with a forbidden cookie. "It's the Francesca Pool. I started this a couple of weeks ago when Sutton and Johnson got into an argument about what she was going to wear the next day. I figured I would set up a little bookmaking. Like I said, just for a little fun."

Francesca was the company receptionist. She had once been a professional model and had the sort of silken hair and soulful eyes that made women grind their teeth when encountering her photo in cosmetic ads. And her comely figure was such that even the most blasé male visitors were known to stammer and trip over their feet when approaching the reception desk.

"You've set up a gambling enterprise based on that young woman's choice of apparel?" I was appalled.

"You bet." He chortled and tucked his wad of money into a zippered pouch. "You want in?"

"I should say not." I lifted my magazine to my face.

"Don't turn it down so fast, Borman. I've got something real exciting coming up. The Great Lingerie Stakes. Bets are now open for her underwear wardrobe. You can back lace underwire bras at six to one. Or there's a long shot — front snap in either blue or red at 25 to one."

I glowered at him from over the top of the magazine.

"Have it your way. It's your loss. So," he said, turning to his pals. "Who's in? White or pink thong panties are almost a cert at three to one."

"Wait a minute." Harding, a meek engineer with an alto voice, held up his hand. "How're we going to know who wins?"

"No problem, boys," Fitzsimmons said. "I've got it all figured out. I'll take the broad out to dinner, connive my way up to her apartment, and when she's distracted, duck into her bedroom and go through her drawers."

Something resembling a dogfight broke out. "Hell no," shouted McCabe. "You can't have a bookie call a race. Plus, I don't trust you as far as...well, as far as I could throw Borman here."

As if with a single mind — which they barely would have had if combined — they turned to me. Fitzsimmons smiled again, this time showing his teeth. "Warren, Warren, Warren," he said, each repetition more insincere. "Seems like you're the only one not in on the pool."

I was unable to believe that anyone — even a man whose idea of fun was to mount a table at the company Christmas Party and display his buttocks — would have the shameless gall to expect me to participate in such an abhorrent scheme. I turned back to my periodical and pretended to be absorbed.

He strode over, sat down, and grabbed the magazine. "Listen, pal," he said in the most conspiratorial voice I had ever heard outside the cinema. "I hear you like to travel."

"Where did you hear that?"

"Everybody says so. All the guys say, 'If there's anybody who likes to travel, it's Borman.' And I'll bet you could use a few extra bucks for that next vacation."

The truth was, I was especially keen on exploring the ancient monasteries of the island of Kynthos. "I don't see what business that is of yours."

"Look here," he whispered, finding and stuffing his mouth with my imported baklava. "You help us on this, and I'll cut you in on a piece of the profits."

"Get thee behind me, Satan." I took back my magazine.

"Five percent, no, let's make it ten percent of the take."

"Ha!"

He bent his foul mouth to my ear. "Last week I took in almost $2,500. The Lingerie Stakes are sure to bring in twice that. How about it for one evening of your life?"

My eyes fell upon the cover of *Travel and Leisure* and the stunning view of the Aegean Sea. Something in me stirred, some primitive passion that overcame my sense of all that is decent. "Twenty percent," I said.

"Fifteen plus expenses and it's a deal. By the way, Borman, that's the worst Pop Tart I've ever tasted.

* * *

Prior to that time I had little social contact with Francesca. In fact, our most intimate interaction occurred one morning after I had over indulged in spiced Bavarian Bratwurst, and she had paged me repeatedly while I was in the lavatory. So, knowing little of the chance that she would accept my invitation, I approached her the next morning.

She was dressed in a form-fitting, low-cut, pink and violet cotton sun dress (ten to one). "Good morning, Mr.

Borman," she said in the mellifluous voice that even over the intercom had made her the object of so many romantic fantasies.

"Good morning, my dear," I said. "I was wondering…"

"Fuerst Quality Products. May I help you?"

For a moment I was baffled until I noticed the thin silver headset she was wearing. "I'm sorry, Mr. Fuerst is in a meeting. May I take a message? All right. Thank you. Now, what can I do for you, Mr. Borman?"

"Well, it so happens that—"

"Yes?"

It struck me that this was turning into more of a challenge than I had anticipated. "It's a matter of dinner."

"Dinner?"

"Why, yes. Exactly."

"What about dinner?"

I couldn't understand why she wasn't catching on. Women of exceptional outward beauty, I recalled, were often lacking in perspicacity. I enunciated precisely so there would be no misunderstanding. "To put it plainly, my dear, would you care to accompany me to a restaurant this evening? I will gladly pay the entire bill." After all, I was being reimbursed.

Her lustrous eyes took on an unexpected light. "Why, Mr. Borman. How sweet of you. I would love to."

I was then aware of a sensation just below the fourth button of my shirt, mildly reminiscent of the time a minuscule braggart knocked the wind from my lungs on the kindergarten playground. It was not merely that this pulchritudinous maiden had accepted my offer. After all, the success of the scheme depended on it. It was the eagerness with which she was looking at me, a look I would have imagined to be reserved for a gentleman a bit younger, and bit thinner and with a bit more hair.

"Yes, well, then," I said.

"Fuerst Quality Products. May I help you?" she said, but not to me.

I steeled my abdomen and began to retreat to the relative safety of my cubicle. "Mr. Borman!" she called. "2120 Pine Street. Apartment 3B."

"Ah," I said.

"Would you pick me up at seven?"

"Ah."

"I can't wait."

"Ah."

That seemed to say it all.

* * *

Having ascertained from Fitzsimmons that my expense account was not to exceed $30, I secured a reservation at Mr. Chow's House of Szechuan. As it turned out, it was unnecessary. When we arrived at 20 minutes past seven the only other patron was Mr. Chow's grandmother, a diminutive relic who lacked a working knowledge of English as well as a working set of teeth.

However much the affair was a purely financial endeavor, I didn't allow that fact to prevent me from thoroughly enjoying the experience. The Moo Shu Pork plate was well worth the $4.95 and, though the decor was gaudy even for a Chinese restaurant, Francesca in her spaghetti-strap black mini-dress (eight to one) brightened the atmosphere considerably.

I quickly learned that one of the secrets to the maintenance of Francesca's hourglass figure was her restricted intake of calories. Although I assured her that the Moo Shu Pork was not to be dismissed lightly, she contented herself with one vegetarian egg roll and a small salad. This allowed me ample scope to reach my spending limit, which I did enthusiastically with the addition of a General Tso's Chicken and a Lake Tung Ting Shrimp.

The first awkward dearth of conversation ended when I asked her why her renowned modeling career had ended. For the rest of our meal, and continuing into the taxi back to her apartment, she went into quite some detail regarding the leering looks, suggestive comments, and inappropriate advances that had been made by men who regarded models simply as expensive prostitutes whose fees were tax deductible.

I began to understand how Fate had saved me from a life of difficulty by endowing me with intellectual rather than physical gifts. Previously, I had no idea of the vicissitudes that Youthful Beauty endured. As Francesca's story progressed, I began to develop a great sympathy for this surprisingly vulnerable and sensitive young woman. The persistent vision of an Hellenic sunset over the Aegean was slowly eroded from my mind by the sultry eyes of my lovely companion.

Therefore when the cab driver, a gentleman who displayed neither a respect for women nor a knowledge of acne medicine, finally took his eyes off his rear view mirror and onto his meter, I came to the conclusion that I could not complete my tawdry mission. I would content myself, in lieu of the Greek islands, with a weekend trip to Newark.

"Mr. Borman," Francesca said, gazing into my eyes in the back seat of the cab. "Would you like to come up for a cup of coffee? It's the least I can do after you've been so nice."

"Well, I..."

Her delicate features took on an expression of ethereal imploration. "My feelings will be hurt if you don't."

"Well, I don't wish to...then again...but of course, my dear. Perhaps just a cup of Premium Sumatra Mandheling Emperor's Blend Decaffeinated if you have any on hand."

I paid the cabbie his due, plus an additional ten cents, which was far too much considering the lurid growling that had accompanied us from the restaurant. Thus it was that I embarked on what would be a momentous interlude.

After fumbling with briefly with her keys, she led me into her apartment. I had barely passed the threshold when she turned and stepped closer. "Mr. Borman... may I call you Warren?"

I was once more aware of a tightening sensation below my rib cage. "Oh, course."

"You may not know this about me, Warren, but I'm a very lonely person."

"No, certainly not you, Francesca."

"Yes, it's true." She was so close that I could smell the egg roll on her breath. "I never had a date in high school."

Having no wish to disparage what was plainly a profound sorrow for her, I refrained from commenting that joining the chess club might have been an adequate substitute, as it had been for me.

"Boys always seemed afraid to ask me out. And the men that I've known, well..." She paused, a brief dark cloud passing across her eyes. "They've never acted very gentlemanly. Not like the way you have. You're really a very special man, Warren."

She was standing so close that her ample bosoms made light contact with my shirt. As what I hoped was a discreet trickle made its way from my right armpit, a quite ungentlemanly thought crossed my mind. "I...I," I said, barely able to speak. "It's...quite nice of you to say so."

In the dim light, her pupils were large and dark and full of the tender gratitude that she was expressing without words. "It was so sweet of you to listen to me go on and on all the way through dinner."

"Ah." Perhaps it was the thought of dinner that brought to the forefront of my mind a sensation that I had been ignoring. "If it would not be too much of an imposition, my dear, might I use your restroom? Huangshan Maofeng green tea always has a powerful diuretic effect on me."

"Why, sure, Warren. It's down at the end of the hall. I'll put on some coffee."

I made my way in the direction she indicated, my legs requiring a stern mustering. The brief contact of our mid sections had thrust me into a tempest of empathy, affection, and arousal. The charms that had launched a thousand improper proposals had finally made me their prisoner.

Then something completely unexpected happened.

The door to the right of the bathroom was slightly ajar. Glancing that way quite casually, I couldn't help but notice it was the bedroom. In the light of the hallway I could see a beautiful Robert Gasparetti four-post bed. However, it wasn't the bed that caught my attention and constricted it in its fist. It was the South American Maple armoire that I was certain held in one of its handcrafted drawers Francesca's undergarments.

My first thought was to take my hand from the knob of the door. My second was to step back out of the room. However, it was my third thought, one much louder and compelling than the first two, that I obeyed. And that was to quickly, cleanly, and absolutely surreptitiously inventory the contents of her most intimate apparel, thus bringing back into the realm of possibility an extraordinary Greek Island vacation.

In three steps my hand was on the brass pull of the top drawer. My intuition had rightly guided me. A pastel array of lace-trimmed gossamer panties lay stacked by a careful hand. I had been instructed to search for thong style garments, thankful that Fitzsimmons had provided me with a rough sketch for identification purposes. Lifting the stack, I quickly identified one white, one black, and one the color of a *hyacinthus orientalis*.

"Warren."

I spun, my entire circulatory system petrifying.

"Warren, I'm afraid a confession is in order."

"I...I don't know what to say."

"I do, Warren. I know what I have to say. It's something I need to get off my chest." I stared at her chest, wondering furiously what it be that she would need to get off of it. "I'm afraid I haven't been totally honest with you," she said.

"You haven't?"

"Oh, Warren!" Even in the dim light I could see a glint of moisture in her eye. "You are such a kind, wonderful man. You've helped restore in me a faith that there are decent men left in this world. I want you to know that I'll never, ever forget you."

"You won't?"

"But I have to confess that in expressing my affection for you, I might have led you to think that there was something more than friendship. Something deeper."

"Well, actually, my dear, I haven't really—"

She clasped her hands and brought them to those famed sensuous lips. "You see, Warren, there's someone else."

"There is?"

"Yes. I'm completely and utterly in love. For the past few weeks I've noticed him waiting for me when I get to work, standing in the corner, watching me like a sweet little puppy dog."

"You don't mean…you couldn't possibly mean…?"

"He works in Research and Development. Maybe you know him. His name is Craig Fitzsimmons. I've been interested in him since the Christmas Party last year. He has the cutest little butt. Hey, Warren, by the way, what are you doing in my bedroom? Why is my underwear drawer open? And what's that you're holding behind your back?"

* * *

"Holy smoke," says the young man in the Dockers. What did you do?"

Warren sighs. "What was there to do? I couldn't bear to crush her innocent infatuation by telling her I was performing a loathsome mission on behalf of the object of her affections. Instead I said nothing and allowed myself to be turned out quickly and severely. Whatever devastating effect my deed had on the poor girl's faith in men, it was nothing compared to the consequences it held for me. As it turned out, Francesca was the favorite niece of Mr. Fuerst. I was let go from my position the next morning."

"Oh, Mr. Borman. That's terrible."

"Well…" A thin smile comes over Warren's face. "It wasn't as bad as it might have been. Upon learning that

Francesca had expressed such enthusiastic partiality toward him, Fitzsimmons immediately abandoned his bookmaking. While I was serving out my notice, I was able to take over his business.

"You don't mean you kept taking bets on the receptionist's clothes?"

Warren gives the young man a contemptuous look. "What sort of person do you take me for? Just the thought is abhorrent. However, I am not a man who isn't able to appreciate a lucrative opportunity. I shrewdly changed the direction of the enterprise to another subject — the duration of the relationship between Francesca and Fitzsimmons. I gave what I thought were generous odds. Marriage, the long shot, went for 125 to one. The lowest odds were three to one for one month."

"Well?" the young man asks.

"Forty-eight hours," says Warren, smiling. "With my winnings and the leisure time afforded me by my period of unemployment, I spent five luxurious weeks touring the Greek islands."

"Wow!"

"My sentiments exactly." Warren reaches behind the young man to switch off his computer that, briefly before it flickers, displays a horse racing form. "Now, in exchange for this valuable lesson, I will ask you to answer my telephone calls for the rest of the afternoon, giving a respectable reason for my absence."

"Absence? Why? Where—?"

"Dover Downs. I plan to put a small bundle on a three-year-old filly in the fifth race. Her name is Francesca."

P Is For Poetry

T he young man in the scarlet and gold Paul Malone tie nearly upsets his office chair at the approach into his cubicle of a slightly older, slight stouter and slightly balder man. "Jeezzus, Warren," the young man says, grasping the edge of his chair. "You shouldn't sneak up on people like that?"

"I beg your pardon," says Warren. "I was merely going to inquire if I might borrow a few sheets of printer paper." He reaches toward the young man's desk but pauses. "From the URL on your browser," he says, "it appears as if you have inadvertently clicked out of the company website."

The young man in the scarlet and gold Paul Malone tie fans the air downward. "Keep it quiet, willya? I've already gotten reprimanded twice this week."

Warren bends closer to the monitor, "StrikeAMatch. com?"

"Don't give me a hard time. It's just a dating site. You might not know this, but it's tough out there for us single guys."

Warren shakes his head and makes a barely audible t'sk. "I'm quite certain it is, but this is dangerous territory upon which you're treading."

"Oh, c'mon. It's not like I'm worried about sexual predators on an adult dating site."

Warren lifts the young man's arm. "If you would be so kind as to allow me to sit down while you locate the printer paper, I'll give you the benefit of my experience, gained at great personal peril."

The young man stands and adjusts his tie. "I don't know, Warren. I'm already in trouble for goofing off on company time."

"Trust me. I will merely be rescuing an employee from a futile search for fulfillment while saving the company wasted employee hours. I only need a few sheets. While you're at it, maybe a dozen.

* * *

You might not credit this, knowing me as well as you do (says Warren), but I entered manhood devoid of an appreciation for the songs of the immortal bards — by that, of course, I mean poetry. True, you might argue, the spirit of the Bormans bends ever toward the aesthetic, but any appreciation I might have had for poetry was snuffed like a cigar in a wet ashtray. At the age of twelve I was obliged to memorize Longfellow's *Wreck of the Hesperus* with the intention of reciting in front of Miss Ruckshank's seventh grade English class. Miss Ruckshank had come to us by way of Montana where she had broken wild stallions for the rodeo, and walked as if she had just dismounted from two weeks in the saddle. I was terrified of both her and the prospect of my assignment.

When the dreaded morning arrived I stood before the class, knees on the verge of buckling, lacking even the briefest notes in the event of a failure of memory. I inhaled twice and began.

It was the schooner Hesperus,
That sailed the wintry sea.

I somehow lurched my way through the rest of the stanza and reached the line :

Her cheeks like the dawn of day
and was on the precipice of
and her bosom white
when I froze.

A torrent of blood rushed to my cheeks at the thought of speaking the word *'bosom'* in front of a classroom of sniggering adolescents, half of whom were not even male. I stammered a whispered *'and her...her...her'* when there arose in my mind a picture of naked breasts that literally seized the attention of my entire body.

"Continue, Warren," prompted the teacher, raising the same eyebrow that could reduce a half-ton of horse flesh to a sorry whimper.

"Her...her..." I had grown used to relying on my razor-sharp intellect, but at that moment, in the midst of a riot of physiological symptoms, my mental faculties completely broke down. I struggled to recall the proper term for that particular part of the female anatomy. *Boobs, jugs, tits, headlights.* None of them sounded like a word Longfellow would have used.

"We're waiting, Warren!" It was likely the entire rest of the school heard the raised voice of Miss Ruckshank.

Knockers, num-nums, cha-chas, ta-tas. I was stymied.

"Warren!"

I knew it was neither *gazongas,* nor *splazoingas,* nor even the euphonic *wop bop-a loo-bops.*

Miss Ruckshank's ruler cracked a sharp whack on the edge of her desk.

I'm ashamed to admit what happened next. The intrusive memories still haunt my restless sleep. Suddenly, and without a polite warning, the contents of my bladder flowed into my trousers. I ran from the room and crouched in a bathroom stall until my mother arrived with a change of wardrobe and a plastic bag. The incident put a bitter end, not only to my appreciation of poetry altogether, but also to any hopes I might have had of ever escaping the taunting of my peers.

From that day on, I avoided even the suggestion of poetry. On hearing the then ubiquitous *'Winston Tastes Good like a Cigarette Should,'* I would cover my ears and click my teeth. I avoided purchasing any greeting cards containing verse, and if I ever received one, would wait until the trembling subsided and tear it to shreds.

Thus I lived in relative happiness until an incident occurred a great many years later that penetrated the fortifications I had erected between me and that despicable literary form.

It began, as many life-altering events do, innocently. One Saturday evening found me at the computer embarking on research into the lost Greek island of Elaia when Google, off the mark as usual, brought up a listing for a web page entitled *"The Languishing Lavender of Elaia."* The first two lines, as sampled by Google, read simply:

The hedonic delection of Elaia's halcyon cascade

Was better than watching Macy's Thankgiving Day Parade.

For some unexplainable reason, I was entranced. I immediately clicked on the link. After registering at the site with my usual ID persona, *fabio_lanzoni,* I was transported to the poet's ephemeral world of words. By the time I reached the 137th and final stanza, I had fallen under the spell of the author, *eulalia_windsong.* Barely able to control my hands, I brought my mouse over the words *The author invites your feedback* and clicked.

What words I invoked at that moment of literary inebriation I have no idea, but *eulalia_windsong* and I began a correspondence that daily raised my spirit from a state of mere existence to one of sublime exaltation.

Eulalia_windsong shared with me samples of her poetry notebook, some so personal and delicate that I blushed even in the privacy of my lonely room. The only thought that marred my otherwise invincible happiness was regret that I had let one single childhood indiscretion rob me of decades of the pleasure of verse. Imagine then my inexpressible delight when *eulalia_windsong* finally revealed that she lived not more than twenty-five miles from my home.

I immediately made plans for us to meet. She suggested the venue be The Dangling Participle, a coffee shop frequented by the local *literati*, but I insisted we dine at Chez Aubergine, the most expensive restaurant of which I was aware. The meeting time was arranged for eight the following Friday. I would know *eulalia_ windsong* by her fine puce lace gown.

The day before our planned rendezvous found me first at the Credit Union, securing a loan for three hundred dollars, next at Freddie's Fine Formals being fitted for a tuxedo, and finally at Fernando's Fashionable Footwear, trying on a pair of dazzling wingtips (with subtle but effective lifts).

Friday I arrived at Chez Aubergine precisely at seven-thirty and, after tipping the maitre'd a dollar, was seated at table overlooking the irrigation spray of the establishment's rose garden. It was a moment only a poet could describe and, taking pen to napkin (regrettably an artistically-folded, fine-count cotton), I began to compose my own verse.

I had just scribbled the line
If I dine with eulalia_windsong
I don't care if I eat with a plastic tong
when I saw a woman come through the entrance wearing

a fine puce lace gown. I dropped my pen in my water glass when I recognized the unmistakable gait — unchanged over the many decades — of a woman who had just come from two weeks astride a horse.

"Ho!" she said, causing a stack of fine crystal on a nearby waiter's tray to tumble. "You Fabio?"

I stood, wondering if even my eighty-five dollar lifts could help. "You're...you're—"

"Eulalia Windsong," she said, thrusting a calloused hand in my face. "Otherwise known as Maxine Ruckshank in civilian life. Say, do I know you?"

"W-Warren Borman," I croaked.

"Hey, pal" she said to a wide-eyed waiter, grabbing him by the seat of his pants. "My mouth's dryer than your grandma's crotch. Get me a boilermaker. Now, where were we?" She plopped herself into the chair. "Warren? Let's see. You by chance ride at the Twisted Buckstrap Rodeo? No. Hey, I got it. Belmont Avenue Junior High."

I admitted I had indeed attended that institution.

"Well, you'll do for a free meal. Warren...Warren...let me think. Aren't you the chubby kid who couldn't finish reciting *Wreck of the Hesperus*?"

My cheeks flushed. I stammered a response in the positive.

"Well, I think it's high time you finished." She picked up her salad fork and pointed toward my throat. "Let's hear it."

"B-but, it's been more than thirty-five years—"

"Then you've had plenty of time to memorize. I expect it to be perfect."

I felt as if I were suddenly a child of twelve. *"Her cheeks like the dawn of day, and her b-b-b..."*

"Her what?" she said in a voice usually reserved for reprimanding bucking broncos. "I can't hear you."

"Her b-b-b..." Then, I'm most ashamed to admit—

* * *

"No!" says the young man in the scarlet and gold Paul Malone tie. "Don't tell me you peed in your pants again."

"I would like to oblige and not tell you that," Warren says, rising from the chair. "But if I do, I would be omitting the climax of the tale."

"You actually peed yourself in this fancy restaurant?"

"The pain of ruining a rented tuxedo and a pair of custom wingtips was offset by avoiding what was sure to be a costly meal. I left in haste, taking with me one of the establishment's fine-count cotton napkins to hide the signs of my shame. That is why, young man, I caution you against the perils of meeting women through the Internet.

At that moment a commanding female voice bursts from an intercom. "You got the corrections done yet?"

The young man straightens his tie and speaks into the microphone. "Er...yeah, Ms. Barker. I mean, I would've had 'em but somebody interrupted me with a story about when he couldn't remember the word for...ah..."

"What are you talking about? The word for what?

The face of the young man takes on a slight hue of the scarlet in his Paul Malone tie. "Ah, the, um…"

"While you're thinking this over," Warren whispers, "I'll take the paper I came to borrow. A ream or two should do. I might just as well borrow your printer, too. It's a much more advanced model than mine."

JOKERS WILD

The young man in the starched white shirt and beige slacks raps lightly on the office cubicle wall with one hand. In his other hand he grips a clump of five-dollar bills. "Hey, Warren," he says. "Got a second?"

The slightly older, slightly stouter, slightly balder man sitting at his computer turns and smiles. "Ah," he says. "I see you've come to offer a contribution."

"Huh?"

"Surely you know I've been trying to collect money toward furthering the work of an amateur archaeologist who is hoping to undertake an expedition to the ancient city of Petra." Warren reaches into his bottom desk drawer and takes out an empty mayonnaise jar. "Just stick the money in here for now. I'll see it gets where it belongs."

The young man in the white starched shirt stiffens. "You don't get it, Warren. I'm not here to *give*. I'm here to *get*. A bunch of us are pitching in to aluminum foil

Ferguson's office while he's on vacation. We figure we need twenty rolls. So how's about five bucks toward supplies?"

For a moment Warren only stares. "And this, you think, will be amusing?"

"Oh, yeah. I saw it done to a guy on TV. They wrapped up everything in foil — his computer, his chair, his phone, even his calendar. It was hysterical."

"Since by 'hysterical' you surely are referring to Webster's definition of 'excessive or uncontrollable emotion such as panic and fear,' I would caution that this is a dangerous undertaking."

"Oh, get off it, Warren. It's just a harmless office prank."

"Harmless? That is precisely the trouble with the world in which we live. People never consider the consequences of their actions. Here, sit down and let me tell you a story about so-called harmless office pranks. When I'm finished you can decide whether you want to do something irresponsible with that money or devote it to furthering the interests of amateur scientific research."

"You're missing the point."

"The point, young man, is exactly what I'm coming to."

* * *

I was at the time (says Warren) in the employment of the E-Z Fit Solenoid Switch Company. The company was struggling against a fierce competitor, Absolutely Superior

Solenoids, and the employees were under severe pressure. Antacids were routinely dispensed in the cafeteria lunch line, and hair loss was becoming commonplace even among female employees.

It was during such a dire period that Lawanda Purvis was hired as Assistant Manager of Packaging and Shipping. Although she flatly refused to attempt this, I was certain that Lawanda could trace her ancestry back to the towering Watusi tribe of Rwanda-Urundi. She was a woman of impressive proportions. When front to front — I in my sensible Rockports and she in her six inch yellow platforms — my eyes were perfectly level with the mid point of her prodigious breasts. I once over-heard Rogers from Engineering, in an uncharacteristic moment of poetic imagery, compare Lawanda's figure to an over-constructed masonry latrine.

From the first moment I laid eyes on Lawanda I was affected by a powerful emotion. For days I was unable to eat or sleep. My every thought was of her. It was a strange, indefinable emotion, not precisely romantic love. It more closely resembled abject fear.

Our first meeting occurred in the company cafeteria. An immense shadow fell across the remains of my Garlic Cajun Prawn Paté on Focaccia. "Hey," she said, settling in beside me. "You're Warren Borman, aren't you?"

I confessed that indeed I was me.

"I've been asking around and everybody says that you're a fun guy."

"They do?"

"Oh, yeah. When I said, 'Who's the most fun guy at this place?,' everybody said, 'Warren Borman.' All at once. It was anonymous."

"It was?"

"Warren, I got to be honest with you. This place is a drag. Nobody has any fun. It's like working in a freakin' morgue. How about you and me livening things up a little?"

"Actually I tend to prefer—"

"Sure you do. Everybody likes a laugh now and then. It boosts morale, and you know what happens when morale gets boosted. Productivity goes up. And when productivity goes up, the company makes more money. Then salaries go up, and we all get to spend more money which helps the world economy. Office pranks are one of the most selfless, autistic things you can do."

Despite the confidence her face displayed in the infallibility of her logic, there were two words — besides 'autistic' — about which I was especially confused.

"Office pranks?"

"You know that guy in charge of Product Development?"

"Brewster?"

"Yeah. A real gum wad if there ever was one. I'm not impressed with those big shoulders. He lifts weights. So what? I've never seen him smile."

I admitted that Brewster was a person of serious demeanor.

"Gimme the name of some important paperwork he might have."

"Pardon?"

"Y'know, paperwork. Important. Name of."

I'm not at my best when put on the spot. "Perhaps a ISO 2001 Requisition for Product Component Vendor Manufacturer Recognition?"

"Oh, yeah. I can tell you're going to be good at this, Warren. Okay, so here's what you're going to do. Write Brewster a note on company letterhead telling him to send a pack of those 2001 Conglomerations to a Helen Back. Don't give him an address where to send it."

I felt a pang of sympathy for the poor woman, physically blessed though she may have been. That sort of prank might send an office of Watusis into fits of laughter, but it wasn't likely to play well at the E-Z Fit Soleniod Switch Company. "I'm afraid all Brewster would have to do is call the Mail Department to get her address."

Lawanda slapped her lengthy thigh and shook with laughter. "Damn right, he will. Just think of it, Warren. He calls up and says, 'I've got a package I need to send to Helen Back.'"

"Ah," I said, beginning to wonder if personnel had acted wisely in hiring this woman.

"Get it, Warren? Helen Back? Hell and back?"

Fortunately, my quick wit rescued me. "I see. It's a play on words."

"What an idiot he'll look like! Once it gets around, this whole place will be rolling in the aisles and you'll be a hero, Warren."

"I will?"

"One small joke for Warren. Giant leap for the company. So how about it?" And with that she leaned so close I had to jerk my head to avoid receiving a blow from her hoop earrings. "Don't let Lawanda down," she whispered.

I couldn't tell if that was a plea or a threat.

* * *

Despite Lawanda's invulnerable confidence, office morale was unchanged the day following our prank. I noticed no one in the aisles, rolling or otherwise. In fact, the only thing different was a pink memo note on my desk when I returned from lunch. It said I missed a call from a Mr. Baer and should return it immediately. So I did.

"I wish to speak to Mr. Baer," I said when the line was answered.

"I'm sorry, he's asleep."

"Asleep?" I was astonished. It was 1:15 p.m. "When do you expect him to be available?"

"Spring," said the young woman. "He's hibernating. So is Mr. Beaver, but I could let you speak to Mr. Buck. He's a real deer."

"Who is this?" I demanded.

"This is the Director of the Mammal House at the City Zoo. Who do you think it is?"

I was unable to answer her question as there arose a cacophony of laughter from the office next to mine. There were about twenty assorted co-workers crowded around a speakerphone. In the center of the group was Brewster — the only person not laughing.

* * *

"Hey, there's Warren. Whatd'ya know?"

I took this as a rhetorical question, as it required far too much time to answer in any comprehensive manner.

Lawanda dropped several coins into a vending machine and pulled the lever with enough force to dislodge every last one of the thousands of empty calories within. "I heard everybody got a kick out of your call to Mr. Bear yesterday."

I straightened myself up in the chair. "The name was spelled—"

"Yeah, sure it was. Anyway, you're doing a great job, Warren. This company is going to owe you big. I wouldn't be surprised if Management isn't already taking notice of what you're doing for them."

"Yes, but—"

"I got something even better. If you thought Helen Back was funny—"

"Well, actually, I—"

"—this is going to be damn hilarious. You know how Brewster always wears white pants?"

"I believe the Testing Lab requires—"

"Ask him to come to your office after lunch. Tell him you want to apologize for the Helen Back stunt. Meanwhile you borrow one of those black chairs from the conference room. Before he gets there you lace the back and seat of the chair with this."

She took a fast glance around the room and extracted from her purse a rectangular plastic bottle. "Toner from the copier," she whispered. "It'll be totally invisible on the chair. Get him to sit down, and when he gets up he'll have black all over his pants and shirt."

I waited patiently for her to continue.

"Don't you get it?" she said finally.

I admitted she had me at a disadvantage.

"He'll get a big laugh out of it."

"But won't that be expensive for him to have cleaned?"

"That's the humor in it, Warren. See? He's got white pants. He sits down, gets up, and suddenly they're black. He might not even know it for a while until somebody says, 'Brewster, your pants and shirt are all black on the back.' Then everybody will laugh."

"They will?"

"Sure. I guarantee it. Laugh their heads off. I just hope somebody from Management is there when it happens so they can see how morale has gone up."

"Won't Brewster be angry?"

"Nah. He'll be glad to find out it won't crack his face if he smiles. I guarantee that he'll be a better, happier Brewster because of it. Trust me, Warren."

And such was the power she held over me that I did. I sent Brewster a message saying I wished to see him immediately. He wasn't particularly pleased. I had interrupted his preparations for Quality Assurance testing and made him walk across the plant merely to accept an apology that I could have given him over the phone. When he rose from the chair, abrupt and annoyed, his backside was covered in black toner.

I spent the rest of the day examining the incident from every angle, trying to discern the humorous element. I gave up in failure.

* * *

When I arrived at work the next morning I found my keyboard, mouse, and phone encased in molded strawberry Jello.

"That's pretty careless of you, Warren, " said Francis in Supply and Purchasing when I submitted my requisition. "You know you're not supposed to have food in your office. We'll have to dock your pay for the replacements."

"Somebody was playing a joke on me," I explained.

"Oh, yeah? Well, I hope whoever did it gets $187.25 worth of laughs out of it because that's what it's going to cost you."

* * *

"I didn't think Brewster had it in him," Lawanda said when she finished laughing. "This is turning out great. Better than I even expected. This isn't such a cesspool of a place to work after all. Wait 'til you hear what we're going to do next.

"We?"

"You know Bobby Pruett?"

Of course everyone knew Bobby Pruett — perhaps not in person, but certainly by reputation. He was at the time the second most popular driver in the FASTCAR racing circuit. Management had signed a contract to sponsor his racecar in exchange for Pruett's endorsement of their products. It was E-Z Fit Solenoid Switches' only hope of competing with Absolutely Superior Solenoids. Their competitor already had the endorsement of the reigning FASTCAR champion.

"You know the company's putting on a big hoo-ha for him at lunch tomorrow," she said. "The press and everything. But guess who's going to be sitting at Pruett's table? That gum wad Brewster. So here's what we're going to do." Her voice took on that now-familiar conspiratorial tone. "Every hear of something called Bag-o-Fart?"

I was forced to admit that my life experience, however varied and deep, did not include knowledge of such a commodity.

"It's just a little thingamabob you stick under some-body's chair and when they sit down, you punch a button on a remote and it blasts this pppf-f-f-f sound and shoots out a smell like whodunit and died. It's funny beyond anything you ever thought was funny. I just happen to have one in my car.

* * *

Settling into a seat that would afford me the fastest exit from the company lunchroom, I watched Bobby Pruett take questions from the few members of the media desperate enough to become pawns of such a painfully obvious marketing ploy. Bobby struck me as the type of young man who, lacking any useful skills, settled for driving a car in circles very quickly. I'm sure that if World Peace depended on someone moving a car a mile in 30 seconds, Bobby Pruett would have been a genuine hero. As it was, he was simply a youngster with a low-grade education, a colorful jacket, and an unintelligible accent.

From context alone I was able to surmise that he was proud to drive a car equipped with E-Z Fit Solenoid Switches — a fact not surprising since the company was paying him a great deal of money to say so. When asked exactly why E-Z Fit Solenoid Switches were better than, say, their competitor's, Bobby shifted his tobacco from cheek to cheek, spat indiscreetly into a glass, and indicated that the question would be answered by someone who actually knew why. That someone was Brewster.

One might expect a fellow with a chest as broad as Brewster's to speak with a commanding voice, but likely years of working in close laboratory quarters had turned him into a mumbler of the highest order. He cleared his throat about two dozen times, and the lady from *Transmission Times* had to ask him to repeat himself at regular fifteen second intervals.

Brewster was apparently proud of something he liked to call the EZSS-2100-M, a product I knew had accrued thousands of dollars in development cost over-runs. He went on about its reliability and so forth and so on and how it could beat the pants off Absolutely Superior Solenoid's ASS-2000-P, the leading product of our competitor.

When the sporadic applause roused me from my near-stupor, I slipped my hand into the pocket where resided the Bag-o-Fart Remote Control. As Brewster made contact with his chair, I pressed the switch.

I have to admit that if there was one flaw with this product, it was that it produced a sound slightly too loud to be plausible. And, with everyone's hearing strained to hear Brewster mumble, the noise was almost deafening. First there was a painfully awkward silence, followed by a small ripple of laughter as Brewster's face reddened, then a collective guffaw as Bobby Pruett waved his napkin in front of his face and raced from the room. The young man couldn't have moved faster had he been in his car.

* * *

Two days later I received a memo demanding my presence before Mr. Farquar, the senior vice president. I had never met him but had been extremely curious ever since hearing from a co-worker that the gentleman had a wooden object lodged in his rectum. However, he betrayed no sign of this disability when I entered his office.

"So, you're a funny guy, Borman."

Hearing this for the second time in a week, I was still surprised, even more so that my reputation had reached Upper Management. I assumed that Lawanda's prediction had come true, that Mr. Farquar wanted to commend me for boosting company morale. Perhaps, I thought, a raise might be in the offing.

"Thank you, sir," I said. "But in all modesty—"

"Well, I fail to see the humor in this." He held up a piece of paper on which there was a photograph of two people in a pose primarily focused on their repro-ductive anatomy. One of the subject's faces had been crudely replaced with that of Mr. Farquar. Underneath the photo was written: IF YOU WANT TO SEE MORE OF THESE, COME TO WARREN BORMAN'S OFFICE AT 4:55 TODAY.

"What do you have to say, Borman?"

I studied the paper. "If I may say so, sir, I wouldn't show this to too many people. Even though the photo manipulation is rather primitive, it might cause embarrassment."

"Show it to too many people? Would you consider every employee in the cafeteria to be too many people?"

I was having trouble understanding why he would ask such a question. "It would depend on the time of day, I imagine," I said. "And, as flattered as I am, I would prefer not to use my office to display your pictures. The space is far too small."

Mr. Farquar's face flushed a color red I had never seen before in a Caucasian. "*My* pictures?" he sputtered.

"This is not *my* picture. This is a despicable, filthy assault on the moral tone of our working environment, not to mention my personal decency. I intend not only to fire you, Borman, but prosecute you to the fullest extent of the law."

It began to dawn on me that a misunderstanding might have arisen. "I think I see what has happened, Mr. Farquar. Someone in a roguish mood has played a joke on the both of us."

"And why would someone want to do that?"

"Office pranks are one of the most selfless, autistic — I mean altruistic — things you can do, sir." I outlined a sequence of events beginning with an embarrassing photo of the company vice president and ending with unlimited economic growth for the entire human race.

"Hogwash," he said. "I'll buy your excuse for now, Borman, but only because I doubt you posses the imagination and gumption to pull off a stunt of this magnitude. But remember," and so saying he thrust a finger at my nose, "I won't forget this."

Neither did the sixty-seven employees who came to my office at 4:55 that afternoon.

* * *

"This joint is jumpin' now," Lawanda said, wiping the tears of laughter from her eyes with my cafeteria napkin. "Can't you just feel the ess-spirit de corpse this company's got?"

I was forced to confess in the negative.

"We got to do something big now, Warren. Something really hilarious. Some giant boot to morale. Hey, I got it." She wrapped her arm around me, dragging my chair toward hers until there was a collision of plastic. "What's the funniest thing you can think of happening to Brewster?"

I considered the matter briefly. "Perhaps we could compose a droll limerick? The possibility of rhyming 'Brewster' with 'rooster' presents several humorous possibilities."

"Hmmm. Good idea, Warren. Let's save it for when we really want to get crazy. For now, I was thinking more like replacing Brewster's prize prototype with a defective one. Think of how funny it will be when he sends it off for quality testing and it fails. Get it, Warren? It fails?" The fact that it was a full thirty seconds before I could interrupt her laughter evidenced how superlatively humorous she considered her idea.

"It seems to me," I finally said, "however comical the results, it would work against the best interests of the company. After all—"

"Warren!" The woman's turquoise painted eyelids rose with incredulity. "You can't be serious? What do you think serves the interests of the company best? Us being stiff-faced sour-pushes or everybody getting down and working their damn hardest because they've just laughed their freakin' heads off? I guarantee you on this one, babe. When Brewster finds out we've replaced his latest model with one of the rejected ones, he'll think it's the cleverest thing we've done yet."

"We?"

"Sure, we. We're in this together, you and me. Come to Momma, Baby." With that, she pulled my head between the Himalayas of her chest to the point my breathing apparatus was attenuated. My final thought, as I lost consciousness, was to beg Dr. Freud for forgiveness.

* * *

The plan, as Lawanda explained it, placed the bulk of the burden on her. As Assistant Manager of Packaging and Shipping, she would exchange Brewster's EZSS-2100-M solenoid prototype with one of the identical defective beta models and ship it to the Quality Testing Lab. The only small, simple step I needed to take was wait until the night watchman had completed his rounds at 2:30 a.m., drive my car up to the plant with my headlights off, mount the fence, cut the barbed wire in a manner that would not be noticed the next morning, locate the correct dumpster and search through it for a disposed model using an infra-red flashlight and night-vision goggles. Nothing, she promised, could be simpler.

So it is no wonder I chaffed considerably when, a few days after I had endured the most physically and emotionally challenging night spent by any mid-level accountant, a notice was placed on the company bulletin board congratulating Brewster for passing the EZSS-2100-M solenoid with flying colors. For this — completely overlooking his exorbitant cost overruns — Brewster was rewarded with a two-week vacation to Bermuda and the company medallion, an embossed tin item that, according to most safety standards, should have required a warning label against possible toddler swallowing.

"Lawanda," I said after corralling her for a discreet moment as she left the building that evening. "I thought—"

She shrugged. "You got me by the sneakers, Warren. Guess I must have got the packages mixed up instead of the other way round. These things happen. Just forget it."

Her nonchalance was astounding. "But what about the joke? What about company morale?"

She stopped walking long enough to examine her ornate fingernails. "Well, to be honest with you, Warren, Brewster's already split the scene, and I think this company's morale is too far gone to be savaged. Well, I got to make tracks. See ya' round the water cooler."

For a moment I watched her sashay toward the parking lot. Then, gathering my wits I started after her, eager for an explanation. Unfortunately, a barbed wire scrape running from my left underarm to the inside of my right thigh prevented me from making any sudden moves. I remained still until she drove out of sight and then went to the drug store to buy more Bactine.

It wasn't that Lawanda had made an error that kept my own morale so low. Even I — should I have cared to examine my life — could likely have discovered I had made a mistake once or perhaps twice. It was the fact that Lawanda seemed to have let her blunder derail her noble effort to save the human race. She seemed to have no more ideas for side-splitting practical jokes. A suggestion of crushed garlic inserted in the mouthpiece of Brewster's telephone was unable to even raise an edge of her heavily lipsticked mouth. The fire was gone.

I spent the most of the following weekend in bed, the shades drawn against the sun. I brooded, not only on the pessimistic outlook for the nation's economy, but largely on Lawanda's transformation from a woman of invincible self-confidence and humor into a somber, hollow shell of her former self.

It was in such a despondent and distracted mood that I listlessly turned through the Sunday paper. My listlessness came to an abrupt end when a banner headline caught my eye:

PRUETT ELIMINATED FROM
GROUNDHOG DAY 200 IN THIRD LAP
MECHANICS BLAME A DEFECTIVE SOLENOID

* * *

The young man in the starched white shirt and beige slacks leans forward in his chair. "No! Don't tell me. That damn woman sent the bad part to the FASTCAR guy instead of the testing lab!"

"Despite your request," says Warren, "that is indeed what I must tell you. Once the source of the trouble was determined to be the EZSS-2100 solenoid, the E-Z Fit Solenoid Switch company was finished. No one bothered to notice that the part in question was the EZSS-2100-F, a discarded effort, and not the Quality Tested version EZSS-2100-M. Monday morning we were told the company was being sold."

"And the woman?"

"She came into my office accompanied by a diminutive man in a three-piece suit whom she introduced as her husband. Apparently her wedding ring had been removed for extensive cleaning.

"She was married the whole time?"

"Mr. Charles Purvis, the father of her six children, was an executive. A financial officer, in fact."

"No! Not with the—"

"Once again I must tell the truth in spite of your plea. He was, indeed, the chief financial strategist for Absolutely Superior Solenoids, the firm that purchased the controlling interest in EZ-Fit Solenoid Switches when the failed company's stock reached five cents a share."

"Damn! What did the woman have to say for herself?"

A slight smile creeps over Warren's face. "Not one word regarding our escapades passed between us. It was only on receiving my severance pay that I felt a sense of, shall we say, closure."

"So she let them sack you anyway. The bitch!"

Warren once again picks up the empty mayonnaise jar. "I would hardly use such a pejorative term. Included with my severance was an extremely generous bonus from the newly acquired company. It was so generous, in fact, that I had the freedom to take several university classes in amateur archeology. Now, are you ready to abandon your dangerous schemes for playing pranks and instead donate that cash to a worthy cause?"

The young man in the starched white shirt and beige slacks stands suddenly. "Hell, no, Warren. That whole story was the biggest pile of bullshit this side of the Mississippi. I don't think they even use solenoids in cars for stock car racing. If you don't want to join in on the fun, too bad, but I'm not giving you one cent. We'll see who gets the last laugh."

With that the young man turns and storms out of Warren's cubicle, unaware of the large black toner stain on his backside.

THE VOICE OF PRUDENCE

"**A**s an assistant bookkeeper, Warren, you must already be aware of the problems facing the company." The man behind the desk with the gold plaque reading CHIEF FINANCIAL OFFICER drums his fingers in the manner of someone anxious to get through an unpleasant situation.

The slightly older, slightly stouter, and slightly balder man on the other side of the desk picks at a tiny wool ball on the sleeve of his sweater. "Well, sir, I don't know what to say."

"There's nothing *to* say," says the man behind the desk, pausing his drumming long enough to pick up a piece of paper. "It's not as if you haven't done good work here. Looking at your qualifications, I'm sure you can find a better job somewhere else. In fact, Warren, I'm surprised you ever settled for this sort of position in the first place."

"Actually," says Warren, "there's a very interesting story behind my decision to join this company."

The finger drumming resumes. "Yes, I'm sure there is. It's just that I have several more—"

"I know you do, sir. That's why I requested your secretary Rosalinda to make conversation with the other poor fellows in the waiting room until we're through. They won't mind a bit. As you know, she has a very agreeable voice."

"You don't understand, Warren."

"But I do, sir. I understand far more than you may realize."

* * *

I had just cashed my final unemployment check from my previous employer (says Warren) and was facing the inevitable drama of the next encounter with my landlady. The woman had developed a bothersome habit of loitering in the hallway with a waiting list of tenants in one hand and a cast iron frying pan in the other.

So, under such pressing circumstance, I responded to a newspaper ad stating that a large firm was then accepting résumés. I brought mine in person with expectations of gaining an advantage. But when I walked into the offices of the financial department and handed it to Rosalinda, I realized I had not gained, but just the reverse. I had lost — lost my heart, utterly and completely.

"*Gracias, señor,*" she said in her sultry Latin accent. "We'll begin interviewing next week." Just seven words — their meaning couldn't have been more mundane — but they were spoken in the most mellifluous voice I had ever heard. With a single sentence, I had been made a prisoner of love.

"I'm sorry, *señorita*," I told her, feigning an onset of momentary deafness. "Would you be so kind as to repeat that?"

"Just call back if you haven't heard from us in a week."

"Call you?" I asked, barely containing my enthusiasm.

"*Sí.* Call me."

And that I did. Every day thereafter. Sometimes two or three times a day. Even when filled with exasperation — which it was most of the time — her voice infused me with a bliss that is impossible to describe.

Then one day my phone rang. "*Hola,* Warren. This is Rosalinda. We have filled the job of senior accountant, but we still have an opening for an assistant bookkeeper. Are you interested?"

"W-would I be working in your department?"

"*Sí.* But the pay is only one half of the senior accountant."

The thought of having to continue to sacrifice gourmet desserts merely for the sake of a keeping a roof over my head flashed across my mind, but only for a moment. A vision of being greeted each morning with Rosalinda's *Buenos días* clinched the decision.

"When do I start?"

* * *

The humiliating experience of having menial tasks foisted upon me by a pimple-faced graduate of a non-accredited community college was more than offset by the sheer pleasure of listening to Rosalinda speculating on embarrassing secrets of other employees around the water cooler. At night I would fantasize I were a bed-ridden patient and she my nurse reading to me the complete works of José Luis Borges. So it was no surprise my knees shook when one afternoon she buzzed me. "*Hola, Warren,*" came the dulcet tones of the voice. "Would you like to go out for a drink after work today?"

"With you?"

"*Sí.*"

"I'll be there pronto," I said, not even worrying that she might expect me to pay.

* * *

Within hours we were ensconced around a table in a local cantina noted for its colored lights and garish décor. I was on the verge of asking her to read the wine list aloud, when her dark eyes suddenly focused on the distance behind me. "Ah, Warren," she crooned. "Do you know *mi amiga* Prudence? Prudence, I would like you to meet Warren. Warren, this is Prudence."

Before I was able to complete the 180 degree turn required by manners, there came a voice so nasal, so abrasive, so like two Styrofoam chests being rubbed together, that I grabbed the table edge for support.

"I've heard so much about you, Warren," was the

meaning I was able to decipher.

I completed my turn to face a slight woman wearing a pair of thick glasses sitting atop a nose that seemed far too small to accommodate the monstrous adenoids her voice suggested.

"Prudence works in our IT department. She is *muy inteligente,* just like you, Warren."

"Oh, Rosalinda, you're exaggerating," the woman said and then lapsed into a sort of chortle that resembled a bullfrog with an artificial larynx.

"And look, here's Ricardo from Engineering. Sit down, Ricky. You, too, Prudence. You don't mind, do you, Warren?"

I was too stunned to speak. This tall, rugged, despicably coiffed engineer used one arm to pull an empty chair from an adjoining table and placed the other around Rosalinda's shoulders. "Yo," he said to me.

A waitress materialized behind me. "May I get you folks something to drink?"

"As a matter of fact," said Rosalinda, "Ricky and I have to get going. His *Tia* Luisa is having something removed from somewhere and we have to take her to the hospital. Don't we, Ricky?"

The pair of them stood up with completely unashamed nonchalance. I was appalled. "You can take Prudence home, Warren, *por favor?*"

"But—"

The engineer winked at me. "Yo," he said.

The rest of the short evening was taken up primarily

by a monologue on my part covering my life from birth to the moment I had ordered the drink in my hand. I talked long, hard, and continuously, petrified that Prudence would speak again. If I had ever complained about the sound of fingernails dragged across a blackboard, I regretted it. I gladly would have traded the voice of Prudence saying, "That's interesting, Warren," for an armada of fingernails across an ocean of blackboards. Somehow I found the strength to endure Prudence's directions to her home as well as her enthusiastic appreciation my company. "Thanks for a great evening," she said when we were parked outside her apartment.

"My pleasure," I lied. "You are a most charming young lady." It was a terrible mistake. She giggled. A kind-hearted fellow pulled up beside us to ask if we were having car trouble.

* * *

"Prudence said that last night was *maravillosa,* Warren." Rosalinda popped her head around the flimsy partition that serves as a wall for assistant bookkeepers. "She's *muy lista* with computers and has a great personality."

"I'm sure she is, or rather, she does."

"The thing is, Warren, Prudence is my very special *amiga.* I wouldn't want anyone to ever hurt her. She's so sweet. And she thinks you're *muy guapo.*"

"Ah," I said with appropriate modesty.

"Are you going to ask her out?"

"Well, I actually hadn't thought—"

"Oh, Warren. It would mean so much to me if you did." Her voice, that voice that flowed like nectar from gossamer clouds, overwhelmed my senses and my sense. "I would be so grateful if you did. I would do anything for you. Anything! "

"What's her extension number?" I asked like a man in a trance.

* * *

"Whats'matter wich you, Warren? Been eating too much cheese again?"

I wasn't surprised that Burgess from Purchasing noticed my distress. Not only was I in the break room holding my head in my hands, but my Belgian chocolate tiramisu torte sat in front of me untouched. I told him I was wrestling with a difficult personal problem.

"Wrestling? I didn't think a guy like you would be interested in wrestling. I got a couple of tickets to the big match I can't use dis weekend down at the Trocadero. You want 'em?"

It was as if an old compact fluorescent bulb switched on in my mind. First, a slight delay, then illumination. My mistake had been to allow my personality to charm this woman. All I needed to do was convince her I was undesirable and she would leave me alone of her own accord. And what could be more undesirable to an intelligent woman than an evening watching muscled men in shiny briefs pretending to hurt each other?

"Sounds fascinating," I said. "I'll accept your offer."
"That'll be thirty-five bucks," said Burgess. "Each."

* * *

Of all the things that could be said about Prudence —
her urgent need for nasal surgery being primary — one
couldn't say she wasn't a good sport. Initially I needed to
explain exactly what a professional wrestling match was
and why its grotesque melodrama was so entertaining —
the latter requiring a great deal of imagination on my part.
But I eventually convinced her the event was one of my
most treasured ways of spending an otherwise perfectly
good evening.

But in hatching my plan, I hadn't calculated on one
thing — my own lack of tolerance for such an abominable
spectacle. Burgess' tickets may have been overpriced, but
they gave us ringside seats, close enough that we were
occasionally dowsed with showers of sweat. That was a
mild inconvenience compared to the howling of the rabble
in the audience, the trembling of the floor, and the roar of
the near-human creatures they referred to as contestants.

I endured it stoically until a man in a striped shirt
announced it would soon be our pleasure to meet the
champeen, a gentleman named Donny Destructo and his
arch-enemy, a youth known as The Masked Mysteriotron.
I excused myself on a plea of needing to use the rest room,
to which I took myself as quickly as possible, dodging
a volley of popcorn and onion rings which were being
hurled at the *champeen.*

In all fairness to myself, I had intended on remaining only long enough to calm my overwrought nervous system. But slumped on the less-than-sterile floor of the men's room was a man holding a brown paper bag who expounded the most extraordinary views on a conspiracy by the Pope, fanatical Zionists and hybrid car manufacturers to fluoridate American breakfast cereals.

By the time I returned to Prudence, the festivities were ending. I apologized energetically and repeatedly, but she seemed distant and subdued. In the welcome but oppressive silence in the cab on the way home, I began to feel guilty for my aversion-therapy scheme. She seemed, after all, a sincere and sensitive soul, and shouldn't be faulted for having the largest set of adenoids east of the Mississippi. When we arrived at her apartment, I went so far as to suggest I wouldn't object to a cup of coffee, but she wouldn't take the hint.

We ended the evening with the limpest of handshakes.

During the rest of the weekend I grew increasingly ridden with guilt. Monday morning I slipped into work early with the cleaning crew to avoid seeing Rosalinda who, I was certain, would have heard the details of my date. I lost count of the number of times I reached for the telephone to dial Prudence in the IT office to apologize. But I was at a loss to put into words the effective sentiment.

At five minutes to five, I resolved to face the woman in person. I had progressed no further than to stand up when I heard what I first took to be a goose being forced into a food processor. It was Prudence. She was standing behind my partition crying.

"My dear woman, what's the matter?" I asked, hoping to quiet her before someone summoned Building Security.

"Oh, W-Warren. W-when you left me alone at the wrestling match..."

I offered her a tissue of which she made maximum use. "It was inexcusable," I said.

"I...I don't know w-what to say."

"Please, my dear, say nothing at all. *Please*."

"L-let me explain, Warren. Right after you left, Donny Destructo came into the ring. The crowd started shouting the meanest, most awful things about the shape of his nose and the size of his ears. It was horrible! Even while he was growling back at them, I could tell that Donny's tiny eyes were filling with tears. Inside that monstrous shaved chest beat the heart of a tender little boy.

"From the first bell, the Masked Mysteriotron was all over him, urged on by that foul crowd. Poor Donny kept taking fake fall after fake fall without mercy. Then, at the end of the third round, the Mysteriotron lifted him by his feet and threw him out of the ring. Donny came down on his back and his head landed in my lap. For one terrible moment, I was afraid he might have broken his neck. 'Wake up, Donny,' I cried. He did.

"When our eyes met, something magical happened. It was as if we had known each other all our lives. The ref was counting him down and out, but all he could say was 'What's your phone number, doll-face?' Yesterday he called and proposed. I've quit my job to become his road manager. We're leaving right after work today. I'm afraid you and I will...will never see each other again."

She pulled me back into my cubicle, took my hand, and stared into my eyes through her industrial strength glasses. "Oh, Warren. I hope you will be brave. I know I must have hurt you intensely, especially after you were so sweet to me. If it weren't for you, I never would have met Donny." She reached for what was left of the tissue and the sound of tortured geese began again. I was afraid her nasal passages were nearing critical mass. "What can I do to make it up to you?" she whined.

I was too stunned to speak. I was still trying to imagine how 'Prudence Destructo' would look on her driver's license when she pushed me aside. "I know," she said. She sat down at my desk and picked up my mouse. "You're linked into the company's financial database, right? Ever heard of VRACORD? It's a neat little utility I installed on the system. Voice Recognition Access Control of Root Directories. Where's your computer's microphone? Oh, here it is. Now just make up a password, Warren and speak clearly."

* * *

The man behind the desk with the gold plaque stops drumming his fingers and puts his hands behind his head. "VRACORD? The root directory of our entire financial database can only be accessed by your voice?

That's a good one, Warren." He laughs. "Everybody says you're a great storyteller, but this one's rich. Really a hoot."

Warren picks again at the fuzz ball on his sweater. "The woman was feeling extremely grateful."

The man behind the desk shakes his head and picks up the phone receiver. "Rosalinda, I know this will sound crazy, but have you ever heard of something called VRACORD? Yeah, VRACORD. Huh? You have? We do? It is? Since when? Oh, no, I just wondered..."

The man puts down the phone and starts drumming on the desk again. "Well, Warren, I don't know what to say."

"There's nothing *to* say," says Warren, rising. "When I see Rosalinda on the way out, I'll ask her to set up a meeting for next week. I think it's time we discussed a promotion."

Stage Flight

The woman in the pink sweater is talking to her co-workers in a voice intended to silence any other conversation in the cafeteria. "Even though I don't like being reminded that I'm turning 40—" She pauses and smiles to provoke laughter. "I want to thank everybody for the presents and especially Miriam for the cake."

Across the room, the slightly older, slightly stouter, and slightly balding man who arrived too late for the festivities looks over at the half-eaten White Chocolate Macadamia Cake with Raspberries and White Chocolate Buttercream.

"Hey, Borman," calls the woman in the pink sweater. "Come over here for a sec." Warren Borman places his napkin over his half-eaten crackers and walks the six yards across the room. His eyes have returned to the cake, causing him to intersect with the edge of a table.

"You didn't get here in time for me to tell you," says

the woman in the pink sweater, "about my Heather's school play."

"Regrettable," he says, taking a seat as close as possible to the dessert.

"It's *Rumpelstiltskin* and I'm selling tickets. Five bucks. Goes to support a class trip for the kids to see *Tubbies on Ice.*

Warren winces. "I'm afraid—"

"Oh, come on," she says. "Everybody else pitched in. It's only a fiver."

"We know you got it, Borman," says a man with a double chin, his mouth still full of cake. "You sure don't spend your money on clothes." The room fills with giggles.

"The issue," Warren says, "has nothing to do with the expense. I find proximity to thespian exhibition, however nascent, to be tantamount to abhorrent."

The woman in the pink sweater scratches her head. "Does that mean you *will* buy a ticket or you *won't?*"

"It means," says Warren, "that I shall explain why the theater is an inappropriate place for children or sane adults."

"Oh, Christ, Borman," says the man with the double chin. "Lunch hour is almost over and none of us can afford to listen... ."

"On the contrary," says Warren. "None of you can afford *not* to listen."

* * *

A great many years ago (says Warren), I had reached the nadir of my struggling career. I was working as a docent at the World Cribbage Hall of Fame in a small mid-western city, known mainly for its strip malls and the smell of rubber manufacturing. The job offered minimal pay and minuscule stimulation. As a consequence, after work I often roamed the streets, searching for meaning in my bleak existence. It was on such a quest that my eyes first fell upon her.

Her diminutive size, almond eyes and Asian front teeth intimated descent from Oriental potentates. One glimpse and I was in the throes of passion, certain our destinies were to become inextricably intertwined. I followed her up three streets and across two avenues. At last she turned down an alley and disappeared though double doors, above which was displayed in large letters, framed by unlit bulbs:

THEATRICKS OR TREATS.

Grooming my hair with a moistened palm I pulled at the knob and stepped inside.

There she was, standing in a dim, pungent lobby talking to a woman whose Amazonian proportions dwarfed my Asian goddess as if the latter were a porcelain figurine.

"So solly," said the China doll. "Auditions tomollow."

Her tiny voice entranced me but her meaning escaped me. "Pardon?"

"Auditions aren't until tomorrow evening, Brainiac," said the Amazon.

"Ah," I said, not being able to evoke a wittier reply. Obviously they had wrongly assumed my intentions. "Yes, well," I said. "Thank you." I stood longer than necessary looking at them, they looking at me. Finally I mustered my knees and began to back toward the door.

"Aren't you going to take a script, Shakespeare?" bellowed the Amazon. "How do you expect to audition if you don't know the play?"

"Ah," I repeated.

The giantess reached into her vast handbag and brought out a stapled blue booklet. *MYTH DEMEANORS,* the cover read. *Written and produced by Pfiona Pflanders.* Beneath the title was a photo of a woman whose jaw seemed capable of removing a bottle cap with a single bite. I looked at the Amazon and then back to the photo. There was no doubt. It was she.

The woman was staring at me as if I were a fungus she had discovered between her toes. Therefore I turned my attention back to the Far Eastern woman, struck by her resemblance to an image I had once seen on a Chinese take-out menu.

She extended a delicate hand and said, "May we."

I was taken aback. "Of course, we may," I said. "Anytime."

"That's her name, Numbskull," said the Amazon. "Mai Wi."

The girl lowered her eyes and bowed slightly. "I am the company dilectol"

"Borman's the name," I said, returning her bow. "But you can call me Wallen."

* * *

I spent the better part of that evening studying the script, weighing the pros and cons of pursuing an involvement with the theater. On one hand there was the script itself — a repulsive posy of puerile versions of all-too familiar myths. On the other hand there was the opportunity to share with the world my latent virtuosity as an actor and, more importantly, an opportunity to pursue a romantic relationship with the inscrutable Mai Wi. It was a brief dilemma.

* * *

"For God's sake, man, put on a shirt!" The entire melange of would-be thespians turned to where I was standing offstage on the following evening, waiting to audition for the role of Adonis. "We'll have the Board of Health close us down for Unsightly Flab Exposure."

It appeared that, as both Playwright and Producer, Pfiona was sole arbiter of fashion, and I was reduced to auditioning in my yellow and white checkered short sleeve seersucker shirt, something I doubted was ever contained in the wardrobe of the original Adonis. Under the circumstances, I couldn't give of my best, and I left the theater despondent, expecting never to see Mai Wi again. So I was astonished when the phone rang the following evening.

"Wallen, this is Mai Wi."

My hand trembled. "Herro," I said. "I mean, hello."

"So solly, Wallen. No Adonis. Too sholt and too frabby."

"No accounting for taste," I said, with a touch of frost.

"But I rike you, Wallen. I want you be stage managel."

"Stage managel? I mean, stage manager? Really? Me?"

"Yes, yes. Okay, okay?"

"Absolutely," I said, brightening considerably. The rush of adrenaline made me lightheaded. "Mai Wi, there is something I would like to ask."

"Okay, okay. Be quick. Many phone carrs to make."

"Would you, that is, will you...may I take you to dinner after rehearsal tomorrow?"

There was a long pause. "You want date?" she said finally.

"Yes, yes," I said.

"Okay, okay, Wallen. I rike you. Arot."

I decided to take that as a compliment.

* * *

The next evening I had barely time to experience the anxiety expected in the hours before a romantic event. Pfiona provided me with list of my responsibilities which included helping with her many costume changes, for it was revealed that she had added Lead Performer to her list of roles.

I began to have a suspicion that Pfiona was not totally satisfied with Mai Wi's choice of stage manager. More than once that evening I overheard her refer to me as "that fat cretin." But my father rightly taught me that one must take the rough with the smooth, so I pulled in my stomach and waited until the end of the rehearsal.

After a rather forceful description of the many failings of the cast and crew by the Author/Producer/Leading Lady, the crowd started to disperse. I found Mai Wi in the dressing room, staring down at her black, round-toed slippers.

"Are you ready to go? I asked.

She looked up at me with what I suspected were moist eyes. "So solly," she said. "No date." I felt as if I had been struck beneath the fourth button of my cardigan. "Pfiona say dilectol no can date stage managel. Confrict of intelest."

As a virgin to the caustic world of theater, I knew no better. "Well, then," I said, "I'll simply resign from my position as stage manager."

She touched my arm. "No, no, Wallen. We need you. I need you."

"But surely you can... ."

She looked up into my eyes, something that women of normal height rarely can do. "I want you to be here," she said. "I want to be crose to you. Prease stay."

"Okay, okay," I said.

* * *

The weeks that followed tested me as I had never been tested. Pfiona Pflanders had a startling ability to detect the slightest personal flaws in any individual and elaborate on them in flowery, nearly poetic form — poetry of the street, that is, interspersed with words that are normally avoided in polite company. She seemed particularly keen on any aspect of me that fell short of her concept of perfection, as both stage manager and a human being. There was an unmistakable gleam of pleasure in her eyes when she would call me to center stage and expound upon my shortcomings in front of the entire ensemble.

But what was far worse was being close to Mai Wi and yet unable to develop a relationship. Whenever our eyes would meet, she would turn hers downward as if it were as difficult for her as it was for me.

There was nothing else but to throw myself whole-heartedly into my responsibilities. The play called for an unending parade of theatrical items that I was expected to hoist and lower with split-second timing. These included cardboard mountains, clouds, temples, and even Pfiona herself in the role of Icarus flying toward a blinking tungsten sun. I doubted if Cirque de Soleil had ever attempted anything as elaborate.

But I endured that period with typical Borman forti-tude, eagerly anticipating the day when the play would end its run and I could again ask Mai Wi for a date. So confident was I that Pfiona's theatrical catastrophe would close after its first performance, I made a reservation for the evening after the premiere at the table nearest the Sauerkraut Bar at my favorite Bavarian restaurant, The Wurst Case. All that was needed was to again put the proposition to Mai Wi.

Thus, an hour before I was to hoist the curtain on opening night of *Myth Demeanors,* I made my way to the closet-like room that served Mai Wi as an office. Even before my hand touched the knob, I heard the unmistakable voice of Pfiona coming from within. She was combining, in a most vigorous and illustrative way, references to functions of bodily elimination with terms describing various aspects of the sex act.

I inhaled deeply and opened the door.

Mai Wi was crouched on the floor, covering her eyes with wet tissues. Looming over her like a German expressionist Mephistopheles with a gland condition, stood Pfiona in her Hades costume, shaking a red-gloved fist.

"Pardon me," I said. "May I have a moment alone with Mai Wi?" Emily Post could not have spoken with more etiquette.

Pfiona, apparently unaffected, turned to me. "Get out," she screamed, "or I'll gouge your eyes with my bare hands." Of course, I could have pointed out that to use her bare hands would have meant removing her gloves, an act that would require some effort as they were sewn into her costume. "And if anything," she continued, veins in her neck as red as her gloves, "and I mean *anything* goes wrong tonight, I'll take a dull scissors and cut off your—" Before she finished her anatomical description, I was already out of earshot.

Many will say that I acted less than bravely. But, as I reflected on the way to my position backstage, it was only a matter of hours until the theatrical fiasco would be over. I would then dry Mai Wi's tears with a frosty mug of *Düssseldorf Roggenbier* and a knuckle of *Aachener Brot*. Together we would refute the assertion that "ne'er the twain shall meet."

Sixty minutes later, I hoisted the curtain to a house half filled with expectant faces, innocent of the assault that was about to be launched on their better natures. But it is said that the Lord works in mysterious ways and in the ninety minutes that followed, He never worked more mysteriously. Everything went off exactly as it was supposed to. The paper maché boulder of Sisyphus (played by Pfiona Pflanders) did not fall off the cardboard mountain as it had in every rehearsal. The foam snow fell upon Persephone (played by Pfiona Pflanders) at just the right speed and not in a lump as it had in every rehearsal. In fact, it was not until Act III, Scene 4 that anything which could possibly be considered amiss occurred.

I had helped Icarus (played by Pfiona Pflanders) into her harness and was waiting in the wing for my cue to turn the winch to begin her flight to the sun. It was then I noticed that the strap which held the harness was caught in the pulley. I climbed a ladder to free it, only to discover to my shock that it had been torn nearly across its width. I knew it would not take much, surely less than the substantial weight of a Pfiona Pflanders, to eventually split it completely, thus letting whatever was hoisted fall a full twenty five feet to its doom.

"And now, rising above all other mortals, I shall begin my ascent," came the forceful voice of Icarus.

It was my cue to start the winch.

"I shall begin my ascent," came the voice again, only a little louder and good bit more caustic.

I came down the ladder, stepped toward the edge of the curtain and met Pfiona's fiery eyes, glaring at me from center stage. Using simple gestures, I explained that a strap had been damaged in the pulley, and if we used the winch she would probably break her neck. For some unexplainable reason, the woman didn't seem to understand. "MY ASCENT! MY ASCENT!" she screamed. Then she thrust her index and middle finger at me, making a movement that was unmistakably that of a dull scissors performing a non-sterile surgical procedure.

* * *

"Holy shit," says the man with the double chin, his mouth falling open to reveal a small portion of White Chocolate Macadamia Cake. "What did you do?"

Warren shrugs. "What else could I do? I hoisted her to full height, locked the winch in place and quickly left by the back door. Then I hastened to my apartment, threw my belongings into a suitcase and took the first Greyhound out of town."

The woman in the pink sweater shakes her head. "I can't believe it. Did you ever find out—?"

"It was many years later," says Warren, "that someone told me he had seen a Pfiona Pflanders on a poster promoting a charity for the handicapped, although I have no idea if it were the same Pfiona Pflanders. As for Mai Wi, she returned to the mainland of her birth and, in the Best Socialist Spirit, opened a chain of highly successful combination theater-gambling casinos for the enjoyment of the Far Eastern proletariat."

"Oh, Christ," says the women in the pink sweater. "Look at the time. It's way past lunch hour." With one swift movement, the entire party, with the exception of Warren, stands and makes toward the door. The woman looks across the tables at the assortment of paper plates, cups, and crumpled napkins.

"Please, don't worry about it," says Warren, placing a firm grip on the plate holding half of a White Chocolate Macadamia Cake. "I'll dispose of everything. It's the least I can do for your birthday."

THE RIGHT CHEMISTRY
PART ONE

"Geez, how come they let the waitresses here wear such short skirts? Don't they know it's hard to concentrate on eating when they're parading around like that?" The young man in the red polo shirt wipes a bead of perspiration off his forehead.

"You wouldn't be so distracted," says the man with the blue sweater, "if you didn't spend the entire meal watching them."

"But look at her. The redhead with the fishnet stockings. I've never seen a woman so beautiful. I'm in love."

The man in the black sports coat chuckles in the way only a married man can. "Yeah, sure. You can tell you're in love just by looking at her legs."

The young man in the red polo shirt turns his head back to his dinner companions. "I'm not exaggerating, fellas. She's the one for me. I'd drive her to Vegas tonight and get married if—"

"If what?" asks the man in the blue sweater. "If you could only work up the guts to talk to her first? What a wuss!"

"Help me, please. I really mean it. Just looking at her makes my knees shaky. What should I do?"

"Get Borman here to introduce you. He's good with the ladies." Everyone at the table laughs. Everyone except the fourth member of the party — a slightly older, slightly stouter, slightly balder man. He brings his napkin to his mouth to hide a smile. "Actually, gentlemen—"

"Just walk over to her," says the man in the blue sweater to the young man in the red polo shirt. "Ask the poor wench if she'd like to have a drink with you after work. What's the worst that can happen?"

The young man in the red polo shirt lets his head drop into his hands. "I couldn't. I'm too nervous."

"Oh, for crying out loud," says the man in the black sports coat. "If it's that bad, let me give you one of my anxiety pills. Put it under your tongue and it'll work immediately. Maybe you should take two."

As the man in the black jacket reaches into his pocket, the slightly older, slightly balder man clears his throat. "I'm afraid benzodiazepines may be an injudicious medicament for amorous diffidence," he says.

"Huh? What?"

"Dispensing a prescription medication without a license is not only illegal, it can have unexpected consequences."

"Christ!" says the man in the blue sweater. "Leave it to Warren Borman to turn everything into a problem."

"It's just some chill pills," says the man in the black sports coat. "Everybody takes them. In fact, ever since the day I got married—"

"Be that as it may," says Warren. "It takes a trained medical professional to prescribe the proper dosage and regimen." He grabs the bottle from the man in the black sports coat. "In fact, if you will permit me to relate an edifying story—"

"Here it comes," says the man in the blue sweater. "Another one of Borman's stories. If I've heard one, I've heard a million of them. It's always some bullshit that winds up with him getting a free drink or a free meal. They're all the same."

"I can assure you—" says Warren, slipping the pill bottle under his napkin.

"Oh, yeah? Well, I can assure *you* something, pal. You're not getting anything out of any of us tonight. In fact, I think it's high time somebody got something back from you." The man in the blue sweater takes the pen provided by the restaurant for signing credit card receipts and starts to write on his napkin. "Before you tell your story, Borman, I'm going to write down exactly what's going to happen. I'll hide it under this plate until you're done. If I'm wrong, I'll pay for everybody's dinner. But if I'm right, you'll not only pay all the tabs, you'll make sure our friend here gets a date with Miss Fishnet. Deal?"

Warren glances at the four checks on the table, his mouth moving as he tallies them. "Upon the unlikely chance of you losing this wager," he finally says to the man in the blue sweater, "will you also agree to be responsible for the matchmaking?"

"Hell, yeah, Borman. I'm so sure of myself, I'll even promise to make sure he gets laid."

Four pairs of eyes turn toward the red haired young woman in the fishnet stockings as she crosses the room carrying an orange glacé cake, a bowl of fresh fruit, and two servings of Dark Chocolate, Plum and Chantilly Millefeuille.

The young man in the red polo shirt lets out a slight whimper. "I don't know, guys—"

"Well, I do," says the man in the blue sweater.

"We shall see," says Warren.

* * *

No family is totally immune from the capriciousness of the genetic roulette wheel (says Warren), and in the Borman family it manifested itself in the form of my cousin Herman. Unlike the rest of our clan who are known far and wide for their gregariousness and charisma, poor Herman was voted 'Most Likely to Cower' by his high school peers. Once, as children, Herman and I were accosted by a department store Santa who invited us to sit on his lap. Herman immediately broke out in a rash and fled home five miles through the snow where he pleaded with his parents to be allowed to convert to Judaism.

However, Nature being on the whole fair-minded, made it up to Herman by blessing him with a phenomenal intellect that he eventually turned toward science and chemistry. During his tenure in graduate school, Herman developed Borman's Booger No More, the enormously successful nasal decongestant, the residual sales of which permitted him to live the life of a recluse, ensconced in his home laboratory. His father, my Uncle Sherman, a former drill-sergeant and tent-revival preacher, worried incessantly about his son and eventually purchased Herman a Russian bride — a charming but totally mute woman whose tongue had once frozen to the top her mouth during a particularly severe Siberian winter. Together, my cousin and his spouse lived the quietest of lives and were eventually blessed with the arrival of a fine son named Thurman.

Over the years I lost touch with Herman, so it was a surprise when I received an invitation to his son's wedding festivities, including dinner the night prior and a bachelor party. Normally, there aren't enough able-bodied horses this side of the Mississippi River to drag me through such an ordeal. But there were two good reasons why I was eager to attend, even though it would require me to spend money on a present that would likely sit in a closet until sufficient time had passed that the couple could put it in a yard sale.

First, I had a fondness for young Thurman who took after his First-Cousin-Once-Removed Warren in good looks and amiable disposition. Secondly — and this was the most compelling — I was eager to see Herman make the speeches that wedding tradition required. I've never been the sort who slows down to gape at a highway accident in the hope of catching a glimpse of a severed limb, but the prospect of Herman standing among a crowd of perhaps hundreds of people and having to say something, if not witty, at least marginally intelligible, was something I couldn't miss.

So, a month later, armed with a gaily-wrapped set of throw pillows embroidered with the portraits of nineteenth-century French *literati,* I arrived at the home of my cousin. Halfway up the walkway I heard an ear-shattering call that sounded remarkably like "HOWDEEEE!"

Looking up, I beheld Herman clad in riding breeches, a ten-gallon hat, and high-heeled snakeskin boots, standing on his roof twirling a rope. "Well, look what Bowser dragged in," he called down. "My fat, bald, misanthropic cousin Warren! Get down on all fours, pard'ner."

"What are you doing, man?" I said, squinting to make sure it was indeed Herman. "You're about to fall."

He did a quick shuffle with his feet and shouted. "Yee-haw! That's just the idea, Cuz. I want to jump from here, mount my proud steed and ride out of town. Only I'm one steed short. You'll have to do. Get down on all fours and run around the house. I'll pick my moment and jump."

"What in blazes is the matter with you, Herman? Come down from there! "

"If you won't co-operate," he said, hooking the lasso of his rope to his studded belt, "I'll simply consider you a proud steed that's rearing on two legs." And he jumped. His aim was perfect and he landed directly on top of me. If it weren't for my wedding gift, which ended up between us and the pavement, vital organs would have been in peril.

As it was, I brushed myself off and demanded the man give me an explanation. After all, we shared the same grandparents and had once been bathed together.

"Chill out, little buckeroo," he said. "Follow and all will be made clear — even to you. You've always been thick-headed, Cousin Warren. I still remember the time you made yourself sick eating three packages of Whip 'n Chill pudding mix."

"I was barely four years old," I said, with not a little asperity.

"You bet. And I see you've been putting on the pounds ever since. Well, no matter. You'll probably die prematurely and the world will be a better, more pleasant place for your absence. Ah, here we are. Go ahead, see if you can squeeze your enormous posterior through the door."

He had led me around the back of his house to where a stairway — far wider than my merely solid frame — led down to a large basement. When Herman turned on the light I saw we were in a highly sophisticated science laboratory outfitted with beakers, Bunsen burners, a menagerie of small animals in cages, and what appeared to be a miniature nuclear particle accelerator.

"Good Lord," I said. "What have you been doing down here all these years?"

He tossed his hat on the skull of a plastic skeleton. "Kind of you to ask, Cuz, but I'm afraid most of it would go over your poor, balding head. Suffice it to say that, where others may have broken the genetic code, I've pieced it back together. Cigar?"

I was appalled. "Certainly not!"

"Have it your way," he said, settling into a chair and putting his feet up on a nearby electron microscope. He lit up and blew a puff of Cuban smoke in my direction. "Here's the short of it, Shorty. I figured out a way to connect artificially altered genes to a fast-acting virus. Once in the system, this concoction completely alters the genetic code of every cell in the organism. In other words, I can change a creature completely."

"Hogwash. You've done no such thing. It's not possible."

Herman took a long puff on his cigar. "Look behind you, Cuz. In that cage on the left. That's Guillermo, an iguana I fed the genes of a parrot. I've had to put a cover over him to stop him from demanding crackers. And next to him is Khalil, a five-year old orangutan. Too bad he's taking a nap. Poor fellow was up all night working on a PowerPoint."

"You're being ridiculous, Herman. But if there were even a modicum of truth in what you say—"

"It's the real deal, Schlemiel. For the last ten minutes you've been talking to living proof."

I was incredulous. The man before me seemed to be in every outer appearance — disregarding the garish costume — my cousin Herman. And yet it was undeniable that he had undergone a dramatic transformation.

"The moment my son and fruit of my loins announced he wanted to tie the matrimonial knot, I panicked. I quivered. I quaked. I knew that I would have to stand up and give a speech. It was absolutely the worst thing I could imagine having to endure. Then it occurred to me: why not find the gene for self-confidence and give myself a swallow? Took a couple of drops yesterday and woke up this morning with an overwhelming desire to become a cowboy."

I watched as he stood up on his chair, beat his chest and crowed.

"But, Herman, are you certain all this is safe?"

"Safety is for jellyfish. I prefer living life on the edge. Oh, damn it, look at the time. I'm going to have to change clothes and drive to the restaurant. Too bad I don't have a plucky thoroughbred to ride. Well, I can't tell you how much I'm looking forward to getting up and toasting my boy at dinner tonight. I'm going to take the opportunity to give his immanent in-laws a good tongue lashing. A couple of stains on the carpet of mankind, if you want to know. I can't see why both their own parents didn't stick them in bags filled with rocks and drop them in the river when they were young. I spent the afternoon compiling a list of their most repugnant characteristics, and I intend on elaborating each of them."

I was becoming concerned for his sanity. "Herman, are you sure that's wise? Think of Thurman. Won't it be awkward for him to sit there while you humiliate the parents of the woman he loves?"

"Just the opposite, pard. I'm sure he'll be grateful I'm straightening them out now, before he has to endure the agony of being related to them."

Before I could warn him that his son might not see things the same way, Herman bounded up the steps taking three at a time. I followed, turning off the lights as I left. After all, the orangutan was still napping.

* * *

I spent the brief drive to the hotel brooding heavily. I had originally anticipated the pleasure of witnessing a tongue-tied Cousin Herman stumble his way through a grueling public-speaking ordeal. Preparing to hear him insult, ridicule and otherwise abuse two perfectly innocent people in an inappropriate forum was a different feeling altogether.

When I arrived at the hotel, I embraced young Thurman and shook the hand of his bride-to-be, a fine lass who was likely unable to help the fact she resembled a Shitzu. She greeted me with an affectionate hug, something I am always appreciative of receiving from females, even those who have markedly canine features. I welcomed her into the Borman family with the utmost sincerity and wished her every happiness, although I was beginning to worry if any girl, no matter how much in love, could stand to marry a man after hearing his father gut her parents like two sardines.

When at last I was introduced to Thurman's future in-laws, I was at a loss to understand why they inspired such loathing in my cousin. They appeared to be pleasant folk who sported mid-western accents and mild manners. The innocence of their demeanor when they filed into the special dinning room seemed unsettling, like beef cattle being herded toward a fast food destiny.

The casual observer might have found little remark-able in Herman's behavior at the table. Only someone who knew him intimately as I would have noticed it odd that he complained to the manager about the heat in the room, then about the draft; that the lighting was too harsh on his wife's complexion, and finally that a song being played by the pianist had been composed by someone with political views Herman found offensive.

When it was apparent most of the food that could be consumed had been, Herman rose, tapped at his water glass until it broke and cleared his throat.

"Ladies and gents," he began in a voice suited more to the arena of a professional hockey match. "I wish to take this auspicious occasion to offer a bit of constructive criticism to a few of the guests who've just stuffed them-selves silly on this overpriced dinner for which I was forced to pay." He reached down under the table and extracted a pile of papers so thick I visibly shuddered.

"But first, I propose a toast to the happy couple. I'm hoping that in drinking to them, my greedy cousin

Warren here will observe some propriety and not guzzle down more than his share. I could tell you a thing or two about what a thoroughly disgusting child he was — and I might yet, as the night is still young. But, speaking of young, let us leave for the moment the overweight and decrepit and turn to the young couple."

"Over the mouth and into the gums," he shouted. He raised a fully-loaded glass over his head and poured the contents down his throat. In the space of about five seconds, he wiped his mouth on his sleeve, belched, licked his lips with his tongue, looked up to the ceiling, rolled his eyes and collapsed in a heap.

* * *

"Oh my God," says the young man in the red polo shirt. "Was he dead?"

"Not even slightly," says Warren. "You see, in his haste to bring his theoretical science into practice, Herman hadn't considered any unexpected consequences. Much of the woes of the modern world can be attributed to just such impatience. As a side effect of his newly-found self-confidence, Herman had developed a complete intolerance for alcohol. He had fallen into a drunken slumber."

The man in the black sports coat scratches his cheek. "I don't get it," he says. "What's the point?"

"There is no point," whines the man in the blue sweater. "There never is a point. Borman just loves to hear himself talk. It's all bullshit, just like I said it would be."

Warren takes a sip of his coffee and leans back in his chair. "From your own impatience," he says, reaching under the tablecloth and loosening his belt, "you have assumed my story is finished."

"It's not?" asks the young man in red polo shirt.

"Not at all," says Warren. "And regarding the point of my narratives, I simply say, 'He who has ears, let him hear.'"

"God help us," says the man in the blue sweater.

"Can I have my anxiety pills back?" asks the man in the black sport coat.

THE RIGHT CHEMISTRY
PART TWO

After we were able to determine the status of my cousin Herman's medical condition (says Warren), his son and I dragged him to a corner of the room and covered him with a tablecloth. Being the next closest male member of the Borman family, the responsibility of giving a toast to the bride and groom fell to me.

Unlike my cousin, I have never shrunk from an opportunity to speak in public. Some of those who know me — although far from all — say I can be highly entertaining. That evening I exceeded even my own standards in holding forth on the virtues of my cousin's only son, pausing only momentarily on an incident when an uncontrolled bowel movement on his part put a damper on the solemn tone of my grandfather's funeral. The lad was two if he was a day and should have known better, but I gave him credit for likely having learned from his mistake.

"I don't care what anybody else said, Cousin Warren," Thurman told me when the revelries had concluded. "I don't think you talked too long. It gave the busboys a chance to get the tables cleared and set up for breakfast. You really have a unique style of speaking your mind."

Modesty forbade me from agreeing with him.

"Listen," he continued, "I want to make sure you're coming to the bachelor party. It's in the Versailles Room downstairs. With Pop being…well, indisposed, I don't have a father figure to be there.

"I'm afraid that parties are not—"

"There's going to be a keg."

"Ah, wonderful. Only domestic beer isn't—"

"And a girl jumping out of a cake."

"A sight not to be missed to be sure, but at my age…"

"If you can't come, I think Great-Aunt Wilhelmina would like to talk to you. She's passing alot of gas and needs someone to drive her home."

I looked into his eyes. They were eager with the blissful prospect of uninterrupted attention to the same woman every day for the rest of his life.

"Perhaps," I said, ignoring the shrill call of Aunt Wilhelmina from the doorway, "I'll join you for just a short while.

* * *

The hotel employee who christened the party venue "The Versailles Room" must have enjoyed a peculiarly sarcastic wit. The area was nothing but an 18-foot by 18-foot section of empty space sectioned off by flimsy partitions. Folding chairs lined the entire perimeter with the exception of a space for a large metal beer dispenser and a table of food digestible only to those under thirty. A well-used banner tacked to the wall read

ALL THE GIRLS ARE REALLY HARRIED
SINCE THURMAN IS GOING TO BE MARRIED

with the word THURMAN inserted with a dry erase marker.

Despite the bleakness of the ambiance, young Thurman seemed determined to make the most of the event and introduced me to his comrades: Jay, Jason, James, Jamie, Jim, Jimmie, and Hymie — all of whom looked well prepared to pretend they were enjoying themselves.

I took it upon myself to expound on a variety of subjects pertinent to the subject of the Married Man, including the correct response to the question, "Do these pants make me look as fat as the brown ones?"

"For a guy who never married, you sure know a lot about women," said Thurman, offering me a piece of fried corn meal containing twice the adult daily requirement of sodium. "Have you ever been in love?"

That, of course, is a question best answered when one has at least several hours to devote to a thorough reply. I had just begun with the tale of Priscilla, the young lady in my pre-school class who seduced me into obtaining for her the entire contents of the teacher's Christmas candy bowl, when there came a raucous noise that faintly resembled music.

Two brief men in white uniforms rolled a cardboard cake about four feet tall into the Versailles Room. For nearly a full minute nothing transpired beyond foot tapping — the youths to the beat of the music, mine in loss of patience. Then, when it seemed as if we were going to spend the rest of the evening staring at each other across a mass of faux chocolate frosting, the object exploded.

Life sometimes reveals itself, not as a random flow of circumstances, but fraught with wisdom. If my cousin Herman had been conscious enough to attend his son's bachelor party, the imagination boggles at what might have transpired. For out of the cake emerged a creature with the head, saddle, tail, and hooves of a horse linked together by a scantily clad female torso that surpassed in splendor anything the Greeks considered the epitome of human form.

It — or rather, she — removed several pieces of frosting from her mane, pranced several times around the room then, announced, "Neigh, neigh, who's the boy whose last free day is today?"

Thurman brought his hand to his chest and the creature trotted over and sat in his lap. In doing so, she made every effort to display the marvelous curves with which nature had endowed her.

Thurman, as he had inherited the well-known Borman

sense of modesty, flushed a spectrum of vermilion hues. Once the boy was utterly and completely humiliated, the creature leapt to her hooves — or rather, her feet — and performed a remarkable dance, demonstrating considerable skill in making her tail twirl in a perfect circle. Finally, synchronized to the final bars of the accompaniment, she removed her headgear, her saddle, her hooves, and her leather bikini top, revealing a sight so indicative of the perfection of Creation that no words can suffice.

After the raucous applause of Thurman, Jay, Jason, James, Jamie, Jim, Jimmie, and Hymie died down, the lass trotted over to the empty chair next to mine, sat, and wiped a dainty hand across her brow.

For a moment I found myself not only unable to speak, but unable to move any part of my body, particularly my eyes. Her face, next to which Helen of Troy would have been mistaken for an Australian blowfish, spoke of a soul with unfathomable depths.

"Hot in here, ain't it?" she said.

Once, in my adolescence, I had been persuaded to trade my last fifty cents at a seaside amusement park for an opportunity to undertake an experience entitled "The Gullet of Hell." After a tedious lift in a rickety chair to the summit, the normal pull of gravity was suddenly replaced by a descent that thrust the entire contents of my stomach into my mouth. It had been years since the incident, but when the lass spoke to me, so without duplicity, so without guile — or, indeed, so without a shirt — I immediately experienced the identical sensation of a lapse of the laws of physics.

When I regained control of my voluntary muscles, I asked if she would like something to drink.

"Sure," she said. "Why not?"

Indeed, what was the objective, existential, underlying postulate that she should refuse? I was flabbergasted at the philosophical implications of her question.

Within moments I had accosted someone — anyone — in a hotel uniform and ordered a glass of the most costly refreshing beverage on the premises.

I hurried back in hopes my seat next to the exquisite goddess were still available. It was. Thurman, Jay, Jason, James, Jamie, Jim, Jimmie, and Hymie were engaged most enthusiastically in the consumption of a low-cost malt beverage and punching each other in the shoulders.

"My dear," I said in my most gallant voice. "You are a consummate terpsichorean."

"Huh?"

"You dance well."

"Gosh thanks, mister, but I wish this was the last time I ever had to do it."

"No!" I was aghast. "But you are a *danseuse premiere.*"

She sighed deeply with the most amazing results. "I really hate bein' a cheap stripper. What I really want to do is style hair."

I brought my hand to my head, ensuring that I

had maximum coverage over the exposed areas of my scalp. "Wonderful! A truly a noble aspiration. Just think where human civilization would be today if we were constantly tripping over our own head growth."

"The thing is," she said. "I'm really a good stylist only..."

I waited for her to continue but her ravishing eyes became lost in the distance.

"Only what, my dear?"

She turned at looked at me with such genuine imploration that I felt a weakness in my legs. "Only on Monday I got to take the state stylist exam to get my license and... and..."

"And?"

"The thing is, everybody says, 'Madeline' — because that's my name — Madeline. They say, 'Madeline, you're too dumb to pass the state stylist exam. You're so dumb, you think a hockey coach has four wheels.' Hey, mister, how many wheels does a hockey coach have anyway?"

I pondered the question. "I'm sure I don't know, either."

"So I guess I got to put on a silly costume, get all cramped in a cardboard cake and flash my knockers for the rest of my life. Or," she added sadly, "until I start to sag."

The tragedy of the situation pierced my heart like a six-inch stiletto. We both sat in contemplative silence until the waiter arrived with her libation.

"Thanks," she said to me, taking a generous gulp.

"Nobody's ever asked me if I wanted a drink before. Most guys only ask me if I want a ride home."

It was at this point, remembering I was merely a guest in town staying with my cousin, that an extraordinary thought occurred to me.

"Madeline, it's possible I may be assistive in your academic dilemma...or, to put it another way, I might be able to help you pass the test."

Her eyes brightened and she sat up straight up — again with delightful results. "Gee, really? That would be awesome. How?"

I scratched my ear. This, I realized, would be a risky endeavor, phrasing the explanation not a small part of its difficulty. "Let's just say that my cousin has invented a line of drinks—"

"Oh, he's a bartender?"

"Well, in a way, my dear. His drinks can alter the way organisms express idiosyncratic genetic psychological traits." My heart was touched by the way her mouth drooped open. "Rather, I think he's got something that can make you smarter."

"Wow," she said. "That would be just the nicest thing anybody ever did for me in my whole life. How much would it cost?"

"Not a thing, my dear. I can arrange for you to have some this very night. By Monday morning you'll be well on your way to becoming a hair stylist."

She suddenly folded her arms over her chest. "Hey,

is this some sleazy way to slip me a knock out?"

"Young lady, I promise you—"

She smiled and touched my hand. "Nah. You don't look like the type."

The type, I assured her, was utterly what I was not.

* * *

In deference to my borderline high blood pressure, Madeline donned a pair of jeans and a T-shirt and we bid farewell to Thurman, Jay, Jason, James, Jamie, Jim, Jimmie, and Hymie. In short order we were entering my cousin Herman's private laboratory, greeted by the merry chirps of the iguana. Fortunately, Herman had the good sense to label his concoctions and it took little time to locate the shelf that held a blue vial marked "IQ."

"What's this goop taste like?" she asked, scrunching her face into the most delightful grimace I had ever beheld.

I found an eyedropper. "I don't think that you'll need much. I hazard that a modicum will suffice."

"You're a nice guy, Warren, but you talk really funny," she said, scratching her luxurious locks with a long-handled Bunsen burner lighter.

I reconsidered.

"Perhaps a nice tumbler full," I said. "Drink up, my dear. I'm sure the bitterness will subside after the first couple of swallows."

* * *

I waited in eager anticipation throughout the rest of the weekend and the following Monday. One minute after five in the afternoon I phoned her but was routed to her voice mail.

"Dearest Madeline," I said. "I was calling to inquire as to the results of your stylist examination and…well, to put it bluntly…to see if I could, ah, in a word, invite you go to dinner with me. I would be most willing — enthusiastic, even — to pay for both meals including the requisite tip. I hope to hear back from you soon. Your faithful servant, Warren Borman."

It was not until Wednesday that I received a postcard.

* * *

"Let me tell you what it said," says the man in the blue sweater. "You gave her too much of the magic potion — or whatever the hell it was supposed to be — and she got so smart, she was too smart for you. I'm dead right, aren't I, Borman?"

"Quite so," says Warren, flagging a passing waitress to refill his cup of coffee. "That is precisely what occurred. Not only did Madeline pass the state examination, but due to the remarkable perspicacity displayed in the essay portion of her test, she was unanimously appointed to preside over the board that set the statewide standards for her profession. In less than twenty minutes after the results were posted, Madeline was offered the position of head stylist at the most prestigious salon in the city.

"The postcard I received went on to express her eternal gratitude for being the agent of her success, but stated that from then on she would only date men who were her intellectual peers, as it would be unfair to trifle with the affections of those who would only end up boring her."

The man in the black sports coat leans back in his chair and begins to chew on the mint-flavored toothpick supplied by the restaurant. "Reminds me a little of *My Fair Lady* only with a bad ending instead of songs."

The man in the blue sweater makes a rude noise in the back of his throat. "Borman's stories *always* turn out bad. It's his way of explaining why he's a loser with women." He turns over the napkin he had written on and reads aloud. "Quote. Borman meets some weird woman and falls in love at first sight. Then, while he's trying to win her over, something goes wrong and in the end he gets dumped. Unquote. Okay, Warren. This time you lose. Pay up, pal. And don't forget you've got to get our buddy fixed up with the broad in the fishnet stockings."

As the man in the blue sweater starts to pass the four dinner receipts, Warren clears his throat. "My friends, once more it appears you have assumed my story is finished."

"Huh? What do you mean? Of course it's over. You got shot down again. You said so yourself. Very funny story, I'm sure, to somebody who's easily amused. But—"

"If you recall, I was, by way of an example, explaining the dangers of misuse of medication. It was not only I, but Madeline as well, who had to live with the consequences of my rash act."

"Speaking of medication," says the man in the black sport coat, "can you give me back my chill pills? My mother-in-law is visiting this week—"

"Can you guys hurry it up a little?" The right leg of the young man in the red polo shirt is moving up and down so vigorously it begins to attract the attention of nearby diners.

"I promise it will be more than worth your while to hear me out to the end," says Warren.

The man in the blue sweater rubs his eyes. "This is a good hour of my life I'll never get back."

THE RIGHT CHEMISTRY
PART THREE

F or several days after receiving Madeline's postcard (says Warren), I couldn't sleep. I tried to erase her memory by the usual methods, but found that even two portions of *Bisque Crèmeuse de Homard et Choux Fleur au Curry* were powerless to diminish my longing.

I drove all the way to her place of work and paced the sidewalk until a representative of the local constabulary accused me of being a potential threat to the community. There comes to many a man a moment when he realizes there exists only one woman for him, and if that woman does not return his attentions he has no option but to resign himself to a life of misery. I therefore mailed applications to monasteries of various persuasions as well as to a six-year, all-male expedition to Antarctica. Regrettably, I was found lacking physically for the latter and spiritually for the former.

Two months later I had lost all hope for life and nearly four and a half pounds. Then it happened — one chilly rain-filled evening when I returned from work planning to dine on a cold can of kidney beans salted only by my tears. I received a palpable shock when, among all the unwanted items in my mailbox, I discovered a letter addressed in a hand I immediately recognized as that of Madeline. I tore open the envelope and read aloud to the emptiness of my lonely apartment.

Dear Warren (wrote Madeline), I hope you will bear the inordinate length of this correspondence, as my narrative might have some bearing upon your own life. At the very least it might enlighten you as to the consequences of the random application of untested chemistry.

As you know, after my examination I immediately secured employment as a *coiffeuse extraordinaire.* Although this was the fulfillment of a long-held dream, I found it somehow intellectually lacking. To amuse myself while executing my daily duties, I developed formulae for such things as calculating the number of hairs on a customer's head in relation to his or her age, head shape, and temperament. I calculated the probability of times the word "like" would be uttered by my co-workers in relation to their highest academic grade completed, the day of the week, and the proximity of their most recent sexual activity.

One day an astonishingly attractive man entered the salon requesting a simple trim. Seeing his corduroy sport coat with leather elbow patches, the unlit pipe he clenched between his teeth, and the four-inch thick book he grasped with his weak, overly manicured hands, I deduced he was a scholar.

My hands trembled when I placed the apron around his neck. For weeks, my romantic fantasies had involved wild, uninhibited passion with a man whose IQ was over 140.

"You don't mind if I read while you work?" he asked with a smile that shot through my heart like pulmonary resuscitation.

I assured him it would not interfere, but my attention was constantly drawn to the material that lay open in his lap. Finally, I could resist no longer.

"Pardon me, sir," I said. "Is that by any chance a book on anomalous covalent bonding in positron emission deterioration?"

He looked up — a move that nearly caused me to shave two millimeters from his left ear. "Why, yes it is," he said with not a little surprise. He turned the book to the cover. It was entitled *Anomalous Covalent Bonding in Positron Emission Deterioration* by Dr. Eunice Barfelmeyer.

I cleared my throat. I'm not the sort of girl who can make easy conversation with a stranger and, never having had the pleasure of attending an institution of higher learning beyond Mr. Bruce's School of Cosmetology, I was unfamiliar with the protocol of addressing a man of learning. "A-a-are you a professor?" I stammered.

He offered his delicate hand. "Richard Head, Ph.D.," he said. "Head of my class in high school, head of my class at Harvard, and now head of the Department of Chemistry at Ivy University. I'm curious, Miss...ah..."

"M-Madeline."

"Well, Madeline, I'm curious why you were so interested in my reading material. Do you know anything about chemistry?"

"Not a thing, Professor," I confessed. "But I was wondering if that little "y" in the formula on the top of page 318..."

"Yes. That's the coefficient. It means—"

"Well, if that funny looking *f*—"

"That stands for "function," which is a term in something called calculus—"

"As I said, I don't know the first thing about chemistry, Professor, but it seems to me that if you use that formula to modify the number underneath the little line—"

"The denominator?"

"...then the multiplication by the coefficient on page 312 would negate the function as defined on page 318 and the result would be a non-real integer."

He examined page 318, then 312, then 318 once again. "Good Lord," he said. "I must inform Professor Barfelmeyer of her mistake. This might change the entire field of non-nutritive food engineering. And you, Madeline — and I say this in the most complementary way — are nothing more than a simple-minded, uneducated hairdresser?"

I admit that his remark brought a blush of shame to my cheeks, already flushed with romantic exhilaration.

I haltingly explained how, even though I enjoyed styling hair, I kept my mind occupied by various methods, which I described.

"Madeline,"' he said with a look of admiration for my intelligence I daresay I received from a potential suitor for the first time in my life. "You are the most extraordinary woman I have ever met. You must consent to have dinner with me tonight or I shall begin to weep uncontrollably."

I told him it would be my pleasure, and so the arrangements were made. At eight precisely he arrived at my door in a dashing mauve three-piece suit and matching faux alligator dress shoes. His hair, of course, was coiffed impeccably, which I say in all modesty.

"Madeline," he said, bowing, "you have me at a disadvantage tonight since, even before I learn more about you, I have lost my heart to you. Never has Divine Wisdom cast such a wealth of intelligence in a vault of such pulchritude. Long have I sought a woman whose mind could keep pace with my own peerless prowess. Now I have found her at last in the form of the most lovely of all God's creatures."

And the evening went on from there, Richard growing more and more poetic until the waiter looked at me from across the room, pointed at my date, and made small circles around his ears. But I considered the server rude and ignorant, such was the intensity of my infatuation with the eminent Professor Head.

At the end of the meal, across a shared plate of *Chocolat du Marnier Suprema,* he took my hand. "Madeline, I can't bear to wait. I want to marry you — tonight. Let's go — nay, haste — to Las Vegas and be man and wife before the sun rises again. Together we will spend our days discussing the non-molecular bonding properties of saline atoms suspended in nucleic solutions."

"Oh, Richard!" I whispered, barely able to speak.

"Call me Dick," he said. "And soon you'll be proud to call yourself my wife — Mrs. Dick Head."

* * *

I don't know if it was the overpriced champagne that Richard — Dick — kept pouring, but I lost all track of time. In a flurry of passion, anticipation, and the reassurance that a man at last was interested in me for my mind, I climbed into Dick's silver Volvo XC90 and we drove into the night. I have no idea how much later it was, hours or days, but at last we exited the highway into a neon world of flash and glitter.

"My dearest, darling Dick," I said. "I can't help but notice we've already passed three All-night Wedding Parlors."

He reached into the glove box and withdrew his pipe, from which he inhaled a non-existent puff. "Ah, *mon petite,* as their name implies, those establishments are open all night. As there are still several hours until sunrise, I suggest we first amuse ourselves at one of the endless casinos that lie before us. And, pulling into the entrance to Genghis Khan's Boudoir, a massive structure in the shape of the Mongolian despot in his underpants, Dick explained the rudiments of a game he called "blackjack."

We soon found ourselves seated in red velvet chairs surrounding a red velvet table being dealt cards by a man in a red velvet suit. "A simple matter, my sweetest," Dick whispered. "All you need to do is watch a few hands, keep track of which cards appear, and calculate the probability of getting as close as possible to twenty-one. When the odds are good, we bet. If not, we don't. With your superior intellect, it should be no problem."

Nor was it. In the space of twenty minutes, we had won $10,000 in chips, something which Dick insisted could be exchanged for legal tender. I was ecstatic. Prior to that moment, I was the sort of girl who considered a five-dollar tip to be a significant step toward her retirement.

"Oh, Love of My Life," I said. "I believe all that champagne has resulted in a call of nature. Will you wait just a moment while I go and powder my nose."

"Huh? Oh, yeah. Sure, sure, anything for you, *mon petit chou chou.*" I kissed the top of his beautiful head while he ran his fingers through the pile of chips.

It couldn't have been five minutes later, as I was leaving the final fifty yards of the palatial Ladies Room, that I heard Dick's voice. He was standing behind a paper maché replica of The Massacre of Constantinople speaking into a cell phone. "Mummsy, it's me, Dickie.

Yeah, I'm in Vegas with the idiot savant. We've already won ten Gs and she's still getting the hang of the game. What? No, of course not. You know they'd kick you and me both out of the social register if I married some twat who cuts hair."

* * *

"Oh, man! That was cruel," says the young man in the red polo shirt. "I had a professor in college just like that. He flunked me just because—"

"So Madeline learned her lesson, I suppose," says the man in the black sports jacket. "That brains aren't everything."

"Precisely," says Warren. "Madeline took the professor's chips and distributed them equitably to a group of senior citizens who were playing slot machines. Then she made an anonymous call to the Las Vegas police department informing them that if they searched the glove box of a silver Volvo XC90 parked in the lot at Genghis Khan's Boudoir, they would find a large quantity of cocaine belonging to the eminent professor Richard Head, Ph.D. I believe the man lost his academic position and now washes windshields for a dollar at busy intersections near the campus."

"So what happened to Madeline?" asks the man in the black sports coat.

Warren sighs and readjusts his belt. "She said that on the long bus ride home she had time to think and realized I was the only man who had ever respected her for who she was. And even though I would never be her intellectual equal, she had brains enough for the two of us."

The man in the blue sweater grimaces and runs his fingers through his hair. "Christ Almighty, Borman! You've told some loopy stories before, but this time you've really outdone yourself. Are you trying to tell us that a young, gorgeous, brilliant stripper came back to you begging?"

"I certainly would hesitate to call it begging. I'd prefer to say the young lady had an epiphany."

"Epiphany? Is that some sort of fit?" asks the young man in the red polo shirt.

"Yeah," says the man in the blue sweater. "She'd have to have had a fit to want to date Borman. So tell us how she dumped you, Warren. And make it snappy. I want to get home before my toddler graduates high school."

"I'm very pleased to tell you gentlemen," says Warren stifling a smile, "Madeline and I were married a year ago this March. I don't wear a ring because of a rare skin allergy."

"Well, how 'bout that?" says the man in the black sport coat as he offers his hand across the table. "Belated congratulations, old pal. I had no idea."

The man in the blue sweater swats his dinner companion across the head with an open hand. "You had no idea because none of this is true. Borman's just bullshitting us so he can make me pay for his dinner. Of course the girl dumped him — if there ever was a

Madeline in the first place. Can't you guys tell a lie when you hear one. Sheesh!"

"Oh, Warren!" All four heads turn at the sound of a melodious feminine voice. Entering the restaurant is a stunning young woman whose perfect figure is interrupted only by a prominent bulge in her midsection. She glides across the room and takes Warren's hand. "Are you ready to go, darling?"

"Certainly, my dear," he says. "How was your shopping?"

"Superb. We finally have everything we need for the nursery. I'm ready for our trip."

The man in the blue sweater tries to talk but isn't able to move his mouth. Instead, the man in the black sport coat asks, "You're going on a trip?"

"Yes," says Warren. "Madeline and I are going to make one last visit to Atlantic City before Warren, Jr. is born."

Madeline steps behind Warren and caresses his chest with her delicate hands. "We always have such a wonderful time together, no matter where we are," she says, her deep eyes gleaming with delight. "Or how much we win."

Warren gathers the four dinner receipts. "I believe these are yours," he says, placing them in the limp hand of the man in the blue sweater. "And I think you might want to make your introduction soon to the young lady in the fishnet stockings."

From beneath his napkin Warren withdraws the small

bottle of tranquilizers "You might want to fortify yourself with a few of these. She seems to be involved in an intimate discussion with that broad-chested gentleman in the motorcycle jacket."

The man in the blue sweater is motionless except for a slight quivering in his lower jaw.

"I only hope," Warren says turning to the young man in the red polo shirt, "that you and the waitress will be as happy as Madeline and I are."

OTHER STORIES

Mixed Messages

Wednesday, February 7 11:40 am
To: maggie.mcleary@ezmail.com
From: d.runkle@oakcrestelementary.edu

Dear Mrs. McLeary,

I have the regrettable task of informing you that I have locked your son, Jamie, in the janitor's closet. He is being punished for bringing to school a color photograph of a woman wearing only red lace underpants and stiletto heels, her legs spread apart and the words "LET'S CELEBRATE HUMP DAY" written across her breasts.

Jamie was in the act of passing the photograph around the lunch table when I intercepted it. I immediately removed Jamie from the cafeteria despite his protest that he hadn't yet eaten his bag lunch — a collection of substances totally devoid of nutritive value. I am hoping that hunger, as well as a few hours in a confined space, may be sufficient punishment to cause remorse.

If not, I may take action to have the boy suspended.

Yours truly,
Dorothy Runkle
Oakcrest Elementary School

Wednesday, February 7, 11:44 am
To: d.runkle@oakcrestelementary.edu
From: maggie.mcleary@ezmail.com

Dear Ms. Runkle,

Boy, am I embarrassed! If you could see me now, you'd see that my face is as red as my panties.

This all began with an article I read in *Parents' Magazine* about what a sweet idea it is to stick a note in with your child's lunch so he can find it when he opens his brown bag. So, I started writing a little message and sending it along every day, something like I WUV YOU, PUPPY or DON'T PICK YOUR NOSE AT THE TABLE.

Jamie seemed to get such a kick out of it, I thought it might be fun to put a note into my husband's lunch, too, only the sort of note that a grown man might like to find in his lunch bag, if you get my drift.

But this morning Jamie let the cat in and she jumped on the counter into Jamie's cereal bowl, which spilled all over his lap. He started crying, so I had to help him find some new clothes, but meanwhile the cat started lapping up the milk, which she's allergic to and she threw up on the floor. While I was in Jamie's room, the bacon began to burn and it set off the smoke alarm, and my husband ran into the kitchen to see what was the matter and slipped on the cat puke and fell on his back.

I guess I must have put the wrong envelope into the wrong bag, or rather the reverse.

So, you see, it's not really Jamie's fault. I think that making him sit alone in a closet all afternoon is simply cruel and unusual punishment, not to mention going without lunch. (Just try to make a five year old's lunch while trying to clean up your husband and get him to Urgent Care.) So, please, Miss Runkle, let Jamie out of the janitor's closet, and I promise this won't happen again.

All the best,
Maggie McLeary

Wednesday, February 7 11:53 am
To: maggie.mcleary@ezmail.com
From: d.runkle@oakcrestelementary.edu

Mrs. McLeary,

Frankly, I'm nothing less than appalled: a) that you would pose for such an indecent photograph; b) that you would permit Jamie to come into contact with such smut; and c) that you would expect me to rescind his punishment. What sort of message would that send to your child?

When an incident like this takes place in an environment that is supposed to be nurturing of moral values — and it is only with a great deal of effort that I am refraining from imagining what Jamie's home environment must be like — it is the responsibility, nay, the duty, of the teacher to take action. It might be too late to help your son, but I must make an example of him for the sake of the other students.

If you were any sort of decent parent, you would see to it that he is punished when he gets home. I think some good old-fashioned corporal punishment is called for, as we are unfortunately not permitted to do so at school.

Wednesday, February 7 12:01 pm
To: d.runkle@oakcrestelementary.edu
From: maggie.mcleary@ezmail.com

Oh, come on now, Miss Runkle. Don't you think you've gone a little over the edge? After all, no harm was done. I'm sure you've done a few things in your life that you've been embarrassed about.

The whole thing is really very funny when you think about it, isn't it?

Wednesday, February 7 12:06 pm
To: maggie.mcleary@ezmail.com
From: d.runkle@oakcrestelementary.edu

"Very funny when you think about it?" Mrs. McLeary, you have a sick, sick sense of humor. I see absolutely nothing humorous in the situation, and if you do (for some perverse reason), I suggest that you are in need of counseling.

I would be happy to arrange a session with you, Jamie, our county psychologist, and a representative from Family Social Services. It might be beneficial in helping you get your life in order, the need of which is apparent from your letters.

I now must get back to class where I intend on giving a lecture entitled "What does the word INAPPROPRIATE mean?"

When the children go to the gym, I am going to scan the photograph, e-mail it to Principal Pearson, and see if he doesn't agree with me that suspension is called for.

Wednesday, February 7 1:06 pm
To: b.pearson@oakcrestelementary.edu
From: maggie.mcleary@ezmail.com
cc: d.runckle@oakcrestelementary.edu

Dear Principal Pearson,

I imagine that by this time you may have gotten an e-mail from Miss Runkle along with an embarrassing photo of yours truly and a request that you suspend my son, Jamie McLeary. Before you make any rash decisions, Mr. Pearson, there are a couple of things you might want to know.

First, there are twenty seven Dorothy Runkles in the US. Three live in our state, but only one lives here in Oakcrest. She's 58 years old, rents an apartment on Windemere Drive, and serves on the administrative board of Cleft-In-The-Rock Freewill Baptist Church, but you probably know all that already.

Here are some interesting trivia facts about some Dorothy Runkles that you might not know:

In 1974, a Dorothy Runkle was expelled from Collins College in Oregon (a state teachers' college) for selling hashish brownies at a Key Club bake sale. She was arrested and released on her own recognizance after being given a suspended sentence.

In 1982, a woman named Dorothy Runkle, then 30, who worked for Quality Electronics in Ohio was charged with misappropriation of funds in connection with a relationship with a Henry Fuerst, a married man and the owner of Quality's direct competition, Fuerst Products. According to the *Akron Beacon Journal* archives, the guilt or innocence of the woman was never established because Miss Runkle jumped bail a week before the trial.

Oh, and I almost forgot. The name "Hot Dot" Runkle appears in the credits for a series of 1970s independent films including GUESS WHO'S COMING AT DINNER, I KNOW WHEN I'M LICKED, and TICKLE MY TUSH.

I thought you might want to check into some of these Dorothy Runkles, especially as your Dorothy Runkle has taken it upon herself to impart moral values to kindergarten students at Oakcrest Elementary.

Wednesday, February 7 1:37 pm
To: maggie.mcleary@ezmail.com
From: b.pearson@oakcrestelementary.edu

Dear Mrs. McLeary,

After receiving your disturbing e-mail, I went to pay a visit to Ms. Runkle. To my surprise, the children told me that when they had returned from the gymnasium, Miss Runkle was not in the classroom. When she did not answer a page, I checked the faculty parking lot and found that her car was gone. This is quite disturbing behavior for one of my staff during school hours.

On my way back to the office, I heard sounds coming from the janitor's closet and discovered that your son, Jamie, had been locked inside. He was unhurt but terribly distraught. I immediately dispatched my secretary to the cafeteria from which she returned with an Icee Chocofruit bar and a bag of Doritos, the sight of which seemed to have an immediate positive effect on him.

I will continue to attempt to contact Miss Runkle, although a call to her home phone resulted only in a message that the line had been disconnected.

I regret any inconvenience to you or your son.

PS: If you and Mr. McLeary ever find yourselves, God forbid, in marital difficulty, I would relish the opportunity to take you to dinner and a movie. Perhaps some Wednesday.

Warmest regards,
Bertram Pearson, Principal
Oakcrest Elementary School

Wednesday, February 7 2:14 pm
From: james.mcleary@ezmail.com
To: maggie.mcleary@ezmail.com

Maggie,

Just had time to grab a bite of lunch. What a wonderful surprise. I wuv you, too, puppy.

My back is feeling much better. Looking forward to celebrating Hump Day!

Love,
James

EVER SO SLIGHTLY MANGLED

For the most part, the houses on Belmont Lane look alike. They are all two stories with barely detached one-car garages at the end of their brief driveways. The owners display their individualities in their choices of paint and fences and flowers, but on the day in question, only one house stood out in marked contrast. On the lawn of Number 609 there was, in no particular arrangement, a brown couch, a green leather armchair, a wicker magazine holder, a glass-top coffee table, a cat tree, a loosely rolled-up mauve carpet and an even more loosely rolled-up ochre carpet pad.

Number 609, with the name Hogan on the dented mailbox, was from where the call had originated. And it was up the rumpled brick walkway to the door of Number 609 where Officer Carmichael went, sidestepping the furniture.

"Good afternoon, Mrs. Hogan," he said to the white-haired lady in the housecoat who answered the door. "I'm

Officer Carmichael. We had a call that someone needed the police."

To Officer Carmichael, Mrs. Hogan looked remarkably like his maternal grandmother, a woman who was prone to smile at the slightest provocation. Unlike the policeman's grandmother, Mrs. Hogan's smile exposed teeth that hadn't the privilege of surrendering to dentures.

"Please come in, Officer," she said, methodically unlatching the screen door. "I'll have to find you somewhere to sit."

The door opened on a flight of stairs and the skeleton of a room, empty but for mauve curtains and exposed carpet strips along the perimeter. "What seems to be the problem, Mrs. Hogan?" he asked, using his standard method of getting to the point.

"It's my handyman, Mr. Mays," she said. She smiled at the policeman and took him by the hand to a small closet beneath the stairs. "Could you help me with these, Officer?" She opened the closet and waved her spotted hand toward two metal folding chairs. "I usually only take them out when I have company."

Officer Carmichael scratched his chin. He was twenty years on the force and knew all too well the irritating confusion between a legitimate need for law enforcement and a simple need for attention. He took the chairs and set them up in the middle of the vacant room. He waited until she sat before taking off his hat and sitting across from her. "What about your handyman, Mrs. Hogan?"

"Mr. Mays?" Her eyes twinkled behind her large trifocals. "He's had such a time working for me! Oh, my, I can't begin to tell you. May I get you some cookies? I'm afraid I can't offer you any milk or tea."

"No, thank you, ma'am. We have some very important cases we're working on down at police headquarters, so we'll have to get right down to your complaint."

"Oh, no, I don't have a complaint. No, not at all. Mr. Mays did his very best. I can't complain about a thing."

"Then I'm not sure what I can do for you, Mrs. Hogan." He stopped his hand from drumming on the edge of the chair seat

She giggled lightly, shakiness the only thing that distinguished it from that of a child. "I suppose I should start from the beginning," she said. "It was my commode. You don't mind me discussing my commode do you?"

If he hadn't been an officer on duty he would have smiled. Instead he said, "Not if it's relevant to your case, ma'am."

"My case! I like that sound of that. That's exactly what this is. It's a case."

"Your commode, Mrs. Hogan?"

"Yes, I only have one. It's in the bathroom upstairs." She giggled again. "Of course it's in the bathroom!"

"Of course."

"You see, over the years the seat — the part you sit on — it had worked its way loose, and I can't fix things myself, so I called Mr. Mays. I got his name out of the phone book. He has the cutest little ad. 'It Pays to Hire Mays.' I don't know if you've seen it."

"No, ma'am."

"You see, I really needed a whole new commode anyway. I told him that when he cracked the bowl trying to loosen the seat. And it couldn't have been more than two or three days until he came back with a replacement."

"Two or three days?"

"At most. Maybe two. Or three, I can't remember. You could ask the Thompsons next door. I'm sure Mr. Thompson could tell you exactly. Oh, that man keeps me laughing, putting a check beside the door every time I came over to use their bathroom. And I know he didn't mean half the things he said." She held her hand to her mouth. "It was just at night, you know, when they locked their doors. Are you too young to know what a bed pan is, Officer?"

"You only have one bathroom, Mrs. Hogan?"

"I said to him, 'Mr. Mays, I think Mr. Thompson has had just about all of me that he can stand for a while. I don't think I can impose on them to take a bath.'"

"What was wrong with your bathtub?"

'My bathtub? Oh, not a thing. It's a fine bathtub. The first thing I thought when Mr. Mays told me about having to turn off my water on account of his breaking a water pipe was that it would be just like when I went off to church camp as a child. I went days without bathing then. Oh, how I hated that part of church camp!"

"He broke a water pipe?"

"Really, the water wasn't off for long. The firemen called him to come fix it."

"The firemen."

"Yes. When I had asked Mr. Mays about taking a bath, he told me that there was probably enough hot water left in my tank for one a bath. He was right."

"What about the firemen?"

"They were so nice. Two young men. One was blonde with an Irish name. Maybe you know him. I told him I didn't know much about electricity, so I really couldn't understand why a hot water heater without water in it could start a fire, but there you go. It can."

"What did Mr. Mays do?"

"Well, he had to turn off the electricity. It simply wasn't safe with all those wires burned. I hardly minded going to bed when it got dark. Just like church camp, only then it didn't get dark so early like it does these days. And there we had kerosene lamps. I told Mr. Mays, I didn't need half the stuff in my refrigerator. Mr. Thompson just loved getting all my frozen steaks. He said it helped make up for Mr. Mays cutting his cable cord by mistake."

Officer Carmichael looked out the window. "Why is your furniture out on your lawn, Mrs. Hogan?"

She giggled again. "Oh, Mr. Mays was nice enough to carry it all outside for me. I was getting my hair done at Gail's. It's that place on Bellevue Street with the potted plants in the window. You probably have seen it. Gail's Cuts and Styles."

The seat of the metal chair was feeling too unyielding for his comfort. "No ma'am, I'm afraid that's not in my precinct."

"Was I surprised when I came home! There must have been eight inches of water on the floor. You see, Mr. Mays forgot that there was an open pipe in the bathroom when he turned on the water before leaving for the day. Oh, my! Well, my furniture and my carpet did need a good cleaning."

Officer Carmichael knew before he looked that there would be a sagging hole in the plaster ceiling.

"Mr. Mays was very apologetic about it. Especially after what happened to Princess."

"Princess?"

"She's my cat. No," she said, the sparkle leaving her eyes. "She *was* my cat. Poor dear."

"So what happened to Princess?"

"Well, Mr. Mays opened up all the windows to help dry out the living room. I know what you're going to ask, Officer. Poor Princess was an inside cat. I suppose she wasn't accustomed to being outdoors. It must have been a terrible fright for her."

The policeman didn't bother to ask another question. He just raised an eyebrow.

"Those big trucks, like the one Mr. Mays drives," she said. "No wonder he has trouble seeing when he's backing up."

"I'm terribly sorry, Mrs. Hogan," he said, standing. "I feel real sorry about what happened to your cat. It's a damn shame. The whole thing is a damn shame, but I'm afraid this isn't a police matter. You might want to get yourself a lawyer."

She looked up at him, her eyes huge and bright behind the window of their lenses. "A lawyer? Piddle! I couldn't afford a lawyer, and besides it doesn't matter now anyway. Not after the accident."

"I'm sure he didn't mean to run over Princess." He put his cap back on and began to fold up his chair.

"No, not that accident, officer. I mean the one when I came home this morning. It was really the silliest thing when you think about it. I just got the gas pedal mixed up with the brake pedal. Right away I knew I must have hurt him very badly because of the way he fell down."

The policeman looked at her again, this time with intent. "You hit Mr. Mays with your car, Mrs. Hogan?"

"He was inside my garage getting a ladder to fix the living room ceiling. It was so dark that it just startled me out of my wits when I suddenly saw a man in the shadows. Then, of course, the sound of it — that terrible thud — that I'm afraid I became terribly rattled. I certainly didn't mean to step on the gas again!"

"So you ran over him after you hit him?"

"As soon as I realized what I had done, I backed up, Officer. Only by that time he was beneath the car. I think that was when I heard him scream. I thought that perhaps he was pinned under the tires, so I went forward again. I guess, looking back on it now, that wasn't the best thing to do. He was quiet after that, though."

Office Carmichael couldn't prevent himself from thinking again about his maternal grandmother. He reached in his pocket for his walkie-talkie and started to call in a Code 30 Henry: Homicide. He decided instead he would call it in as a simple Code 20F: Fatal Accident.

"You'll have to take me to see Mr. Mays, Mrs. Hogan. After that I'm afraid I'm going to have to take you down to the police station, but first let's get all your furniture back inside," he said smiling.

THE MIRACULOUS POWERS OF MISSY MCKINNICK

"Bless me, Father, for I have sinned. It's been three months since my last confession."

"That's a long time between confessions, young lady."

"I'm sorry, Father. Mom brings us every week, but I've been hiding in the choir loft."

"And your mother doesn't notice?"

"There's too many of us for her to keep straight, Father."

Father Paul rubbed his hand across his cheek. "You must be one of the McKinnick kids."

"Missy, Father."

"The little one who always wears a pink dress?"

"That's Katy. She's too young for confession."

"Ah," said Father Paul, reluctant to further violate the secrecy of the confessional. "So why do you hide in the choir loft, Missy?"

There was a silence in the darkness.

"Missy?"

"I've been scared to come to confession, Father. I've been so bad. I'm an evil person."

Hearing confession, in spite of its requirement for the faithful, was the most onerous sacrament for Father Paul. He was uncomfortable being cramped for hours in a dark closet, a pretense of anonymity between himself and his parishioners. There was rarely anything to engage his attention. Husbands who were involved in blatant extra-marital affairs spoke simply of losing their tempers with their children. Physically abusive alcoholics owned up only to falling asleep during mass. Children were the worst with their endless recounts of teasing their siblings or tormenting their pets.

"Now what would make you think you're evil, Missy?"

More silence.

"You're not allowed to tell anybody what I tell you, are you, Father?"

"No, I'm not. Whatever you tell me is going to be between you, me and God."

"Well, it may have been God who started it. I don't really know. I'm hoping you can tell me."

"First I need to know is what you've done that makes you think you're a bad person, Missy."

"Do you remember last summer when I was really sick?"

"Of course," he said, comfortable that it was not the first lie to be told in his confessional.

"I had a real high fever. I couldn't even come to Mass."

"That doesn't make you an evil person."

"That's not it, Father. You see, when I had this real high fever, I dreamed that a man came to me."

"A man?" he asked, suddenly alert to how he might reconcile the confidentiality of the confessional with a responsibility to report child abuse. "What sort of man?"

"He had a beard and was dressed in a robe. Like Jesus, but it wasn't Jesus. I think it might have been one of the disciples."

"Ah," he said, only slightly disappointed.

"He told me I was special. That I had special powers."

"What sort of powers?"

"He didn't say, but when I woke up, Michael came into my room and started jumping on my bed."

Father Paul struggled to suppress his impatience. He knew there was a line of the penitent outside the confessional. "Yes?"

"Well, I wanted him to leave, so I thought real hard and said — just in my head — Michael, stop jumping on my bed and go over to Patrick's house. And he did, even though it was raining."

"Maybe you really said it out loud, and your fever made you think it was in your head."

"No, Father. Even if I had said it — which I didn't — he wouldn't have done it. I made him do it. It was the Power the disciple in my dream was talking about."

"Now, Missy…"

"Then I tried it on Mom a couple of days later. She was yelling at all of us about not doing our chores."

"God wants us to honor our father and mother."

"You don't understand. I told Mom in my head to stop yelling about the kitchen and call out for pizza. You know what she said, Father? She said, 'Hells bells. I give up. You just do what you want. I'm going to call out for pizza.' But I didn't make her say 'hells bells.' That was her idea. Maybe she already went to confession about that."

A smile crept across Father Paul's face. "I'll bet that's not the first time your mother's called out for pizza."

"It wasn't Mom. It was me. I did it with the Power."

"Missy, listen to me..."

"Then, on the first day of school I made Sister Sharon sit me in the back of the room, right next to Molly. Molly's my best friend."

"Missy..."

"I keep trying to tell you, Father. You're not getting it." There was a current of petulance forming in her voice.

"Please listen to me for a moment, dear. God gives children a special blessing. It's called imagination. It helps children to expand their minds and be creative. It's a gift. No, it's a power. That's what the disciple in your dream was talking about. He was talking about the power of imagination."

He could hear a small but definite groan.

"I'm not dumb, Father. I know what imaginary is, and this isn't imaginary. I sat in the back of the room thinking, Pick up the chalk, Sister Sharon. Now roll it around in your hands. Now put it back down. Now scratch your nose. And she did all those things. I'm not lying, Father. There was chalk all over her nose. Everybody started to giggle. I did it. I made her do it. That's why I was afraid to come to confession. I'm evil. I'm an evil person."

Father Paul let his head fall into his hands. He felt a slight throbbing in his temples. "You haven't made anyone do anything bad have you?"

"No, but what if I do? I can, you know. I've been doing it to my Mom and Dad and Sister Sharon and even Molly. I could make anyone do anything, even if it were the baddest thing in the world. What if the disciple in my dream was really Judas?

"You aren't an evil person, dear. You're just a child. Just say three Hail Marys…"

"You don't believe me, do you, Father."

Father Paul had a vocational abhorrence to anything belonging to the dim world of the metaphysical. But — and the word crossed his mind in spite of his rational determination — his religion bid him to believe many things that were contrary to reason. "I believe that you believe it, Missy. If you like, I'll say a special prayer for you. Just say three Hail Marys…"

"What if I prove it to you, Father?"

"Prove what?"

"What if I prove to you that I can make people do things?"

"Now how would you do that?"

There was another silence.

"Missy, really."

"Okay. What if I make you do something?"

"What would you make me do?"

"I'm not going to tell you. If I told you, you might be able to keep yourself from doing it. You're a priest, you know."

He tried to squint through the slats that separated him from the girl. "Then how would I know you were making me do it?"

"Oh, you'll know, Father. Someday I'll come to Mass — you know we always sit up front — and I'll make you do something funny. It'll be something everybody'll laugh at. You'll see. I'll make you believe me."

"Okay, he said, despite an unwelcome tightness forming in his stomach. "You make sure you come back to confession when your mother brings you next week. No more hiding in the choir loft. For your penance, I'd like you to say three Hail Marys, and now make a good Act of Contrition."

For a long moment Missy said nothing and he shuffled his feet, fiercely resisting the reminder that not all his actions were safely conscious.

"Oh, my God," she began, "I am heartily sorry for having offended Thee, and I detest all my sins…"

He listened closely. Her words were precise. Yet by the tone of her voice he could tell she was smiling, almost as if she were smirking, as if she knew something about which he was afraid to imagine.

THE MAN WHO INVENTED POLKA-DOTS

April 17, 1894

Eleanor and I checked into the *Hôtel Merveilleuxe* in Paris this afternoon. When the clerk noticed my name on the guest register, he threw his arms into the air so vigorously the *postiche* covering his bald pate nearly loosened from its mooring. "S*acreblu!*" he exclaimed. "Ees it really *vous*?"

I assured him that I, indeed, was myself. He began exclaiming, *"Le petit pois! Le petit pois!"* This burst of enthusiasm attracted the attention not only of the proletariat behind the counter, but of the *bourgeoisie* nibbling *Camembert le Rustique* and sipping *Pessac-Léognan* in *le Grande Foyer*.

A silver-haired woman who couldn't have been more than five feet tall grabbed my sleeve. "Dear Monsieur," she squeaked, "I met you when we were in New York last *automne*. Do you remember?"

"I could never forget such a lovely lady," I said with a gallant bow. Disingenuousness has become *de rigeur* for us *galant* celebrities. "It is wonderful to see you again, Madame."

"Did you hear that, Pierre?" she said to her husband, who was cupping his hand to his ear to catch our conversation. "I told you we were friends."

"*Oui!*" the deaf buzzard replied. "I *know* we are in France!"

The crowd did not allow us to continue this entrancing *repartee*, as an apparently unending river of bereted Frenchmen flooded in, begging for my autograph on whatever scrap of paper, cloth, or *crêpe* they could find.

So much for our hope of escaping the limelight on the Continent.

May 25, 1894
We crossed the Channel incognito yesterday, I in the guise of a bespectacled Mandarin laundryman and Eleanor a pregnant Scandinavian wet nurse. After disembarking, we took the train to Paddington Station where I was struck by the sight of what appeared to be a royal retinue. "*Ah so*, Svetna," I called to Eleanor, speaking through my false buckteeth. "It appears as if some of the alistocracy are travering by lail."

We tried to skirt the crowd, hoping to catch a lorry to our hotel, when who should emerge from the throng but Albert, Prince of Wales. I recognized him at once from his likeness on the tinned tobacco. "Hoy!" he cried.

"Thought you could use the old bespectacled Mandarin laundryman wheeze to give us the slip, old bean?"

"Your Royal Highness," I said, lowering slightly on one knee, "I should have known that no mere fancy dress could fool a true Englishman. You have me by rights."

"Mum wanted to tag along," he said, by way of reference to Her Royal Highness. "But she's sitting on the head of the Prime Minister over some sort of trouble in the Falklands. But no matter. Look here, there's something that I *must* show you."

And with that, he took me by the arm and carried me across the station to the public loo. Waving away his entourage of dukes, marquises, barts, and M.B.E.s, he pushed me through the small door marked GENTLEMEN. I was quite taken aback when he slipped off the Royal Belt and dropped the Royal Trousers. "What do you think?" he asked, doubtlessly pleased with himself beyond punch.

"Quite fetching, my dear Prince," I stammered, for the Royal Silk Drawers displayed a stunning gold on blue pattern. One of my very best, I thought, and I told him so.

"I knew it had to be. They were a gift from the little woman," he said. "Got it last Guy Fawkes Day. Had a matching tie, but I spilled roly-poly pudding on it." He cast me a sympathetic glance. "Quite sorry, old chap. Couldn't be avoided."

I was about to assure him these things happen when the door swung open and a stringy fellow in a visor brandishing a notepad thrust himself into the cubicle. "Meeks," he said by way of a hoarse cockney introduction. *"The Times.* Could we getyer to pose fer a pictyer, Yer 'Ighness?"

Before Prince Albert could answer, in strode, in this order, a three-legged wooden stand, a black hooded contraption the size of a small potting shed, and what was indubitably the photographer, a gaunt midget with an overgrowth of side-whiskers. "Make yerselves comf'able, blokes," he said, brandishing a flash disk the size of gladiator's shield. "You won't have to hold your pose for more than five or ten."

By this morning, my likeness was on the front page.

June 24, 1894
How sweet the smell of good old American air! We've spent the past five days aboard the *Pride of Columbia,* I as a paraplegic Portuguese toreador, Eleanor as a fair-haired Ethiopian soothsayer. I literally leapt from my wheelchair upon descending the plank and kissed the very soil of the land of the free. To ease the astonishment of my fellow passengers, I attributed the apparent miracle to the primitive but efficacious magic of my dark-skinned traveling companion.

We were met at the door of the apartment by Mrs. Apple. What a red, white, and blue Yankee Doodle daughter! Born of sturdy New Jersey stock, she is ever faithful in her service to her employers, whether they be traveling in some exotic land or within arm's reach, pestering her to accommodate their most picayune American desires.

"Howdee, Boss," she said, greeting me with a crushing handshake at the threshold. "Sure got a haystack of mail while you were gallivantin' around the world." True to her word, she produced a pitchfork and began nicking away at pile of envelopes the size of a generous haystack. All of them opened, I noticed.

"Bless you, Mrs. Apple," I said while Eleanor went off to the powder room to remove five days worth of boot black from her face. "Once again you've proved the faithful family retainer. What does my public have to say?"

"Mostly the usual, Boss." I didn't need to inquire further. Indecent proposals from women of all ages, solicitations to endorse ineffective products, politicians vying to be seen with me to bolster flagging careers. It was all quite touching.

"But here are a couple you might want to take a gander at," she said, handing me an elegant embossed, robin's egg blue envelope and a tattered, barely legible scrap, apparently hand folded from used packing material. I pulled out the former.

"Bully, bully!" I exclaimed. "Tell Eleanor not to unpack. We've been invited to the Vanderbilts along the Hudson for a *soirée*. Vandy says plenty of other swells will be there whooping it up."

The other envelope bore a foreign postmark. "Whatcher think?" asked Mrs. Apple.

"Nothing to be concerned about," I reassured her after giving it the once-over. "This sort of crank claim happens invariably to an inventor." The missive was from a man in

Slovenia who claimed to have preceded my famous invention by twelve years. "Improvable assertions abound. Any Tom, Dick, or Ljubljana can say they invented the steamboat, but only Fulton brought it to fruition. That's why we have patent offices. Dismiss any concern from your mind, Mrs. Apple. As soon as Eleanor is a Caucasian once more, we shall depart for upstate."

June 28, 1894

What a day this has been! After a rousing game of polo with Vanderbilt and an afternoon jaunt grouse hunting with Rockefeller, Eleanor and I sipped pleasant beverages with the complement of the company on the veranda. We were enjoying the magnificent vista and the cool of the evening when Alexander Bell and Tom Edison clustered 'round, eager to press me for advice. "In my book, old man," said Bell, strapping an arm around my shoulder, "you're nothing shy of an inspired genius."

"I believe," Edison interrupted, "that inspiration is only one percent genius."

I couldn't help but notice the tiny beads of sweat on his broad forehead. "The other ninety-nine percent must then be perspiration," I said.

The entire crowd laughed heartily, but I noticed Edison jotting down my remark on his cocktail napkin.

Then the letter arrived.

It was brought to me on a gold salver by one of Vanderbilt's foot servants. In a large brown envelope was a telegram that had been forwarded by Mrs. Apple. Reading it, I began to totter.

"Are you quite all right?" asked Edison.

"Fine, fine," I lied. "Please excuse me, dear friends. I must depart your company and douse my temples with rose water." I made my way to an inconspicuous corner behind a thirty-foot *Bianco Trani* Ionic column and wept like an infant.

August 4, 1894
It has been over three weeks since the news surfaced that the daughter of the Slovenian had registered his invention with patent offices in Austria, Prussia, Spain, the United Kingdom, as well as several East European principalities with unpronounceable names. Documents have been produced that not only prove his invention predated mine by a dozen years, but also suggest I filched his design from a menu in a Croatian beanery on 43rd street.

A week ago Monday I took a cab downtown to see my boyhood chum and personal attorney, Fitzhugh McPatrick, hoping to bring legal action against those parties attempting to besmirch my good name. He looked me up and down and tugged at his beard. "Faith and begorrah!" he muttered, the potato in his mouth muffling his brogue. "I've a stack of lawsuits agin ye as tall as the Blarney Stone. Copyright violations from sixteen countries. Attemptin' to fraud the US patent office. Crossin' state lines with an equivocal fabric pattern. I have only two pieces of advice for ye, laddie. First is to settle 'em all out of court. Second is to find yerself a new lawyer. I quit!"

Tuesday my trusted business vendor, Hymie Rabinowitz of Rabinowitz, Wabinoritz, Barinotiwz, and Zabinowirt Clothiers, dropped by unexpectedly while I was in the midst of my mid-morning bath. "You *shlemiel!*" he shouted, entering the bathroom and yanking the drain plug. "You've botched the whole *shmeer*! Your contract is a *shmatteh!*" He told me that, under the circumstances, he and his brothers had chosen to go with solids and stripes only for their fall line. Monies owed to me, including all royalties and residuals, would be diverted to compensate them for losses and retooling expenses.

Wednesday we received word from our realtor that our offers for the house in the Hamptons, the seaside resort in Florida, and the investment property in Atlantic City had been rejected due to my "insufficient resources and scurrilous reputation."

Thursday our landlord informed us that the lease on our Upper East Side apartment had been suddenly and irrevocably terminated. Eleanor and I were required to evacuate the premises by the end of the month. We were spared the inconvenience of having to move our furniture by a group of burly Armenians, hired by my banker brother-in-law to help offset our debts by seizing our personal property.

When the final tabulations were made on Friday, our liabilities exceeded our assets by fourteen dollars and seventeen cents. Even the sandwich that had been given my name by a famous Philadelphia delicatessen was changed to simply "the hamburger."

Thanks to the generosity of the ever-faithful Mrs. Apple, we are now sharing a third-floor tenement in Hoboken with her sickly aunt and fourteen obese cousins. Eleanor, the dear soul, has taken work with a Catholic orphanage, inspecting heads of indigent children for lice. I awaken every morning to a day of cleansing pigeon droppings from the sidewalks of Hoboken.

Hope, however, springs eternal. Yesterday while in the park I stopped to observe a pair of octogenarians playing a game of checkers. Staring at the board, I began to envision a new kind of design — based on the red and black playing board, but utilizing white and red alternating squares. I can see it now gracing tablecloths in Italian restaurants. I have already begun to work on some preliminary sketches. I think I may call it "paisley."

DIETING WITH JESUS

Dear Plaid Press,

I am inquiring if you would be interested in publishing a book of mine entitled *Dieting with Jesus*. It describes a method for losing weight based on New Testament Scripture. This book is sure to quickly become a bestseller and a big money maker for Plaid Press.

Sincerely,
Reverend Curtis Fuller

Dear Reverend Fuller,

We are interested in learning more about your book, *Dieting with Jesus*. As you may know, books on Christian topics are very popular now, and dieting books have been a staple with the American reading public for many decades. It is, however, customary in non-fiction book proposals for the author to include an outline or perhaps a table of contents of his work. I am curious how you have woven your subjects together.

Regards,
Howard Plum, Acquisitions Editor
Plaid Press

PS: You may want to check your writing for split infinitives.

Dear Mr. Plum,

Here is the table of contents for the book that I have been working on. Thank you for the suggestion. This will certainly make writing the book much easier. The following list is by no means complete, just something to begin with.

The Lamb of God: Hold the mint jelly!
Jesus in the Dessert: Get thou behind me, Satan!
The Fish and the Loaves: Divide, not multiply!
Wine into Water: A calorie-saving miracle!
The Last Supper: Braking the bread!
Walking on Water: 30 minutes a day to a new you!

Sincerely,
Reverend Fuller

Dear Reverend Fuller,

Thank you for sending us your table of contents. However, before we make a decision regarding any non-fiction book proposal, we like to know the credentials of the author. Please tell us about yourself and your qualifications to write this book.

Regards,
Howard Plum, Acquisitions Editor
Plaid Press

PS: You may want to check your writing for sentences ending in prepositions.

Dear Mr. Plum,

As a Baptist minister and the son of a Methodist minister, you couldn't find anyone more qualified to write a book like this. However, the divinity school I attended, Charismatic College of California, is no longer in existence, having had it's accreditation revoked.

I have spent many years in churches, several of them behind the pulpit. If you would like a personal reference, you may contact Mrs. Mildred Cricket, the former wife of the deacon of the last church where I was pastor. She can be contacted at the same address you use to reach me.

I have an unparalleled knowledge of Scripture, especially *Psalms* 32:1, *Proverbs* 17:28, and *Romans* 7:24.

Sincerely,
Curtis

Dear Reverend Fuller,

In these days of tightening budgets for publishing houses, it has become increasingly important for authors to assume responsibility for their own publicity. If we were to publish your book, it would be necessary for you to go on an extended author's tour, lecturing and holding book-signing events. The tour might also include television appearances.

Would you be able to take time away from your current responsibilities to go on such a trip?

Regards,
Howard Plum, Acquisitions Editor
Plaid Press

PS: You may want to check your writing for dangling modifiers and the correct form of the possessive for the word it.

Dear Mr. Plum,

Their is no one more willing to hit the road and lecture than me, as I am currently in between church assignments. However, I must confess that with all the idol time I have had (mentally, of course, working very much diligently on my book), I have let myself go a bit. Right now I am two hundred ten which is a bit over the desired wait for a man of my height (five two). I hope this won't be a problem, especially considering this is a diet book.

Sincerely,
Your pal, Curt

Dear Reverend Fuller,

I am pleased to inform you that Plaid Press has agreed to publish *Dieting with Jesus*. We have a sub-editor who will develop a book outline and a very talented team of ghostwriters to complete the manuscript. In addition, our in-house publicist will construct a list of impressive credentials for you and elicit celebrity testimonials. We even have contracted with an outside talent agency to hire a slim, attractive actor to stand in for you on the book tour.

Please find attached our standard author contract. As an advance on your royalties, I have enclosed a check for $50,000 and a copy of the *Chicago Manual of Style*.

Regards,
Howard Plum, Acquisitions Editor
Plaid Press

www.ingramcontent.com/pod-product-compliance
Lightning Source LLC
Chambersburg PA
CBHW070105260626
47160CB00004B/1324